"Something's scanning us, burning out all my instruments," said the pilot of the plane.

"But down there is where I gotta be, Harry!" Wolverine told the pilot as he tightened the straps of his parachute. "Thanks for the lift!" And with that, he was gone, plummeting earthward.

The sound of his parachute opening drew the attention of the Phalanx unit called Larissa. "What?" she gasped.

"Heads up, circuit-face!" Wolverine yelled, his bone claws extended for business. "The ol' Canucklehead is back in town, and somebody's gonna pay!"

Wolverine slashed his claws across the techno-organic neck, severing the head. "You stick yer mug where it don't belong, it's gonna get ripped!" he shouted.

But from the neck grew several long tentacles, each with a hideous head on its end! They wrapped themselves around Wolverine, squeezing so tightly he could hardly breathe.

"If that is the best you can do, mutant, then this entity of Phalanx will make short work of you!"

Catch all the X-MEN books:

Sprinter X-Men® Novels

Sabretooth Unleashed
Cyclops & Phoenix

Coming Soon...
Upstarts Uprising
Gambit: Unfinished Business

Bullseye X-Men® Novels

Days of Future Past
Second Genesis
Wolverine: Top Secret
The Xavier Files
The Brood
X-Men in the Savage Land
X-Tinction Agenda
Wolverine: Duty and Honor

Super Edition: The Phalanx Covenant

THE PHALANX
COVENANT

adapted by Paul Mantell and Avery Hart

based on comics by Scott Lobdell, Fabian
Nicieza, Todd DeZago and Larry Hama

cover illustration by Steve Lightle

text illustrations by John K. Snyder III

Bullseye Books

Random House 🏠 New York

A BULLSEYE BOOK™ PUBLISHED BY RANDOM HOUSE, INC.

Library of Congress Catalog Card Number: 94-074053
ISBN: 0-679-87160-8
RL: 4.5

First Bullseye edition: October 1995
Manufactured in the United States of America   10 9 8 7 6 5 4 3 2 1

⊗ ⊗ **Prologue** ⊗ ⊗

Gambit had never seen anything like it before. The huge beast seemed to be neither human nor machine—maybe both. It had already trashed a posh New York City nightclub—and now it was out on the street, looking to do more damage.

Luckily, Gambit had arrived just in time to stop the thing. Not so luckily, it had now turned its attention to him.

Most times, Gambit traveled with a full deck of cards in his pocket. When he charged them with his mutant power and threw them, they exploded with the force of a bomb. But tonight, he found himself caught short—down to his last four cards!

He had already tossed one at the ugly beast. Sure enough, the explosion made a mess of the creature's techno-organic body. But a few seconds later, it began to pull itself back together somehow—even bigger and more powerful than it was before!

"Uh-oh," Gambit muttered under his breath. He'd always been a master thief. Maybe now was the time to steal out of here...

Gambit looked around for a way out. But his motorcycle was blocked from behind by a line of traffic that snaked down a one-way street leading to downtown New York City.

"Your act of desperation was as pathetic as it was fruitless, Gambit!" the creature said in a scratchy, mechanical voice.

Gambit's jaw dropped. It knew his name! Then, before he could react, a techno-organic tentacle whipped out and grabbed his motor-cycle from underneath him! Before Gambit could pick himself up from the ground, the thing had absorbed his bike!

"Once we have assimilated the mass from your mode of transportation, we will be that much stronger, more powerful. Such is the way of the Phalanx, for we are constantly adapting. Already, our internal technology is preparing to counter your biogenetic charge!"

The creature advanced toward him, its tentacles raised and grabbed him.

"So, tell me, Sparky," Gambit said casually, in the Cajun accent he'd picked up as a youth in New Orleans. "You pretty much absorb everyt'ing, *non*?" Behind him, the horns honked in the stalled traffic. "Yo, robot-man," Gambit said, "I got news for you. Aside from swallowing de metal, rubber, and leather, you gulped down de gasoline, too. Flammable gasoline—all it needs is a little spark. And I happen to have an ace up my sleeve..."

The card flashed. The ball of flame went up, and when it died down, there was nothing left of the surprised Phalanx unit but ashes.

As for Gambit, he was on his way back to X-Men headquarters in Westchester County— by public transportation.

Phalanx...That was what the thing had called itself.

Gambit had never heard the name before. But he was sure of one thing: now that he had heard it, he would never forget it.

1

It was the following week, on a Saturday night at about nine o'clock, when the X-Men got the call.

"Attention, X-Men," the mechanical voice on the speaker called out. "Incoming call on priority circuits. Come to the main control panel immediately."

"It's Professor X!" Psylocke said. The powerful telepath looked intently at her comrades. "Let's go!"

The X-Men followed her into the X-

Mansion's high-tech control room, crammed with state-of-the-art computers and telecommunications gear.

"I know he's only been on Muir Island a little over a week," Bishop said hopefully, "but perhaps he's already found a cure for the Legacy Virus!"

The professor had gone to Muir Island, near Scotland, to work at Dr. Moira McTaggart's Mutant Research Institute. There, they were trying to find a cure for the deadly Legacy Virus, which had attacked mutants worldwide.

"Get outta town!" Jubilee said, rolling her eyes. She was the youngest of the X-Men, still a teenager. "He just got over there, Bish. Nobody's gonna cure that virus overnight."

"What's bothering you, Jubilee?" Bishop replied seriously. "You've been down for a while. Is it Wolverine?"

Jubilee sighed. "I miss him, Bish. He was my best friend. Why did he leave, anyway? Do you think he'll ever come back to us?"

"Wolverine felt he was no use to the X-Men without his adamantium skeleton," Storm explained.

"It makes sense," Iceman interjected, "after his fight with Magneto. Having adamantium ripped out of my insides would sure take the fight out of me! I wouldn't blame him if he decided to quit and retire to Canada."

"Wolveroonie'll be back. I know he will," Jubilee insisted. "At least, I hope so. Anyway, as for Professor X, he's probably just callin' to say hello. "

"On the priority circuit?" Archangel pointed out. "I don't think so." Even though his metallic wings were tucked back behind his blue shoulders, they almost nicked Beast as the X-Men gathered by the monitor.

"Er, watch those feathers, Warren," Beast warned him. "I'd hate to get brushed by one. It would require numerous stitches to repair."

"Take it easy, Hank," Archangel replied. "The scar would never show under that blue fur of yours."

As they arrived at the main control bank, they were joined by Rogue and Gambit. *Those two have been seeing a lot of each other lately,* Storm thought.

Two of the original X-Men, Cyclops and Jean Grey, had just gotten married and gone off on their honeymoon. Storm wondered if all that romance had rubbed off on Rogue and Gambit.

All these thoughts fled Storm's mind as Professor Xavier's face appeared on the monitor. She saw at once that his expression was unusually anxious.

"Greetings to you," he said. "Where's Banshee?"

"Away for the weekend," Archangel replied. "I think he had some old friends he wanted to look up in Massachusetts."

"All right," Professor X said. "But my message cannot wait. I've picked up some disturbing psi-signals here on Muir Island. An alien thought pattern, and yet human, too. I can't quite pin it down."

Storm looked over at Gambit. She wondered if the signals the professor was describing could have come from the strange creature Gambit had met up with last week—the one called Phalanx...

"To make matters worse," Professor X went on, "the other mutant teams—X-Factor, X-Force, and Excalibur—have been sent on important missions since Jean and Scott's wedding. Only Moira and I are here if a threat materializes."

"Do you want us to join you and Moira on Muir Island?" Storm asked. As leader of the team, she was already mentally preparing herself for battle.

"I'll go get the Blackbird ready for flight," Bishop volunteered.

"Not so fast, all of you," Professor X cautioned. "I'm afraid that your coming here may not be a good idea. In fact, it may not even be possible."

"I don't understand, Professor," Storm said.

"I'm picking up the same alien psi-signals from inside the X-Mansion," Professor X explained. "I'm afraid you may be—"

Suddenly, the transmission shorted out and all they could hear was static.

"Are you thinking what I'm thinking?" Storm asked Gambit as the others looked on.

"I think I'm thinkin' what you're thinkin'," Gambit replied ominously. "Phalanx."

"I sure wish Wolvie were here," Jubilee said nervously.

"And Scott and Jean's presence would be most useful, too," Beast added. "So would

Banshee's. Unfortunately, we shall have to make do with those of us still present."

"I'm sure," Storm said, "that with our combined powers we will be able to overcome any atta—"

At that instant, a giant tentacle whipped out from behind the bank of controls and wrapped itself tightly around her neck. She was lifted off the floor. Storm wanted to use her power to control the elements to defend herself, but she was too busy gasping for air.

Looking around desperately for help, she saw Beast's entire head being covered with coiled tentacles. "Mphmpmph!" he cried out.

"Stormy! Look out!" Jubilee called as the writhing techno-organic tendrils advanced toward her. Jubilee turned and ran from the room, screaming and beating off tentacles as she escaped.

It seemed that the very walls of the X-Mansion were alive with Phalanx invaders!

"Gambit!" Iceman called out as they both tried to fight off the onslaught. "You never said anything about how gross these creatures were, pal!"

"Forgive me, *mon ami*," Gambit managed

to reply before he was overwhelmed by the dozens of tentacles that engulfed him. "I'm a t'ief, not a poet."

"Can't you throw some cards at them?" Rogue wondered.

"Sorry, *chère*. You can only use a trick once on these fellas. I advise you to—" His words were suddenly cut off as a tentacle covered his mouth.

Iceman tried freezing his attackers. It worked—for an instant. But then the Phalanx units adjusted to his powers, developing an instant resistance to them! Iceman was done for.

They were all done for.

Storm knew that she couldn't hold out much longer. She could no longer see her companions—only the techno-organic micro-circuits growing under the green humanlike skin of the tentacles that smothered her face, cutting off her breathing.

And then, she heard the scratchy, mechanical voices of the Phalanx units.

"Submerge into ether matrix...go digital... set protocols...send data...transfer to Phalanx core...request permission to download data."

"Core central...this is Comrade Unit Hodge...relay your request, remote unit 2."

"Regarding primary objective...takeover of X-Mansion well under way. Majority of X-Men already apprehended. Operation proceeding as planned. Clones ready to take their positions..."

"Proceed along present parameters, remote unit. Well done. Will prepare for X-Men's arrival at core central."

Those were the last words she heard. Storm lost consciousness, knowing that the battle was over.

The Phalanx had arrived.

2

Sean Cassidy, known to the X-Men as Banshee, stood looking down at Emma Frost. She was strapped in with strong restraints, which held her down on the bed in the X-Mansion's ultramodern medical unit. Her hands and head were enclosed in adamantium casings to keep her from using her telekinetic and psionic powers.

Emma—the so-called White Queen—had been cured by Professor X quite recently. Now she was at the mansion, recovering from the yearlong coma she'd been in since the death of her mutant students, the Hellions.

The X-Men had always regarded Emma Frost as an evil mutant—certainly she'd been one of their opponents. But Banshee knew better than to judge a person by his or her past.

During his life, he'd been an Interpol agent in Europe, Lord and Master of Cassidy in Ireland, a police detective in New York City, a reluctant villain in Nashville, and, finally, a globe-hopping mutant crusader. He knew from personal experience that people could, and often did, change.

Perhaps it was not too late for the White Queen to make a new start in life.

"Ye really should calm down, lass," Banshee was telling her in his lilting brogue. "No one here is trying t'hurt ye." He glanced over to the room's control bank, where Storm and Iceman were monitoring the readouts, their backs to him.

"Hurt me?" Emma Frost echoed loudly. "They're trying to kill me, Cassidy! Storm, Iceman, Archangel—all of them—they're afraid of me! They know if I wasn't restrained,

I could read their minds! I could ruin their plans...I could destroy them all!"

"I'm certain ye could, Ms. Frost," Banshee said gently. "I'm certain ye could."

He did not share his private thoughts with her. Clearly the poor woman was having delusions. It was obvious that the strain of losing her Hellions was having an effect.

"But ye must remember," he went on soothingly, "ye were in a coma for almost a year—'tis important to understand what kind of stress that placed on your mind and body."

The White Queen writhed in a vain effort to free herself. "This isn't about me, you idiot!" she shouted. "I can't tell exactly what's wrong—can't even think clearly during these 'tests' they've been running on me—but something is wrong. I know..."

Suddenly, she fell back onto her headrest, her eyes glazed over. Banshee looked up at Storm and Iceman. "What happened to her?" he asked. "It's like she was cut off."

"Sonic disrupter field, Sean," Iceman replied, without looking away from the control bank. "Unlike you, we've been hearing her freak for the past three hours."

"Yes," Storm agreed. "We could all use a break."

"Now do us all a favor," Iceman said to Emma Frost as he went over to her bed. She raised her head to protest, but he reached above her and hit the sensor buttons. Her head dropped back down onto the headrest. "Lie there and be quiet."

Banshee frowned. He didn't want to be butting his nose into the day-to-day decisions. Still, he couldn't help feeling that Iceman and Storm were perhaps not the ideal candidates to run the diagnostics on Emma Frost.

Both of them had had bad experiences with the White Queen in the past. She'd even taken over Iceman's body for a while. But what could he say so they wouldn't be offended?

"Storm," he began, "if I might have a word with ye?" Drawing her aside, he said, "I cannae help thinking that in light o' their recent history, Bobby being here might be adding to Emma's confusion. If ye'd like to take him somewhere—talk about his feelings—I'd be happy to finish these readings."

"Very generous, Sean," Storm replied. "But

unnecessary. While you were tending to other matters, Charles left very specific instructions before he left for Muir Island. And you know," she added with a smile, "I'd never disobey Professor Xavier."

"Well," Banshee said, "I suppose the professor knew what he was doing. But—"

"But nothing, Sean!" Storm cut him off. "No one knows more about behavioral psychology than Professor X. No doubt he believes it is important for Bobby and Emma to deal with each other—rather than let bad feelings get worse!"

"But—"

"You'll see, Sean," she insisted, hustling him out into the hallway. "Unwind from your trip, shower, get a good night's sleep, and by morning, everything will be fine."

"But—"

"Sean...trust me." She gave him a look that startled him—a look he'd never seen in her eyes before. "Come sunrise, you won't have a care in the world."

Slowly, he backed off. "If yuir sure'n ye don't need any help?" But she had already turned and shut the door in his face!

"I should probably go back in there and argue me point," he said to himself. "But face it, Sean...ye're definitely out of your league around here.

"'Tis me own fault, really," he went on as he walked back down the hallway. "How long has it been since I've shown any true commitment to the X-Men—since I've felt that this place has been a home?"

Nothing had been the same since he'd left to find his own true love—Moira McTaggart—only to discover she wasn't sure how she felt about him anymore.

Not exactly a healthy relationship, he reflected sadly. Ah, well—maybe it was time to accept that if he was to be any use to his fellow mutants, it would have to be somewhere else.

Suddenly, there was a buzzing noise on the screen above him. A message flashed in orange: INCOMING CALL—PRIORITY FREQUENCY.

"What?" he said aloud. "An incoming call on the priority frequency? I should probably let one of the full-timers handle this. I dinnae want to be overstepping me—aach! Listen to me! Carrying on as if me feelings are hurt, just because Storm dinnae take me advice. Not *too* sensitive, eh?"

As it turned out, the call was from Scott Summers and Jean Grey. "We're about to return from our honeymoon, Banshee," Scott informed him, "and we're looking for Professor Xavier."

"What's it all about?" Banshee asked, curious.

"We don't have time to explain," Jean said quickly. "But believe me—it's urgent."

"Well," Banshee told them, "the professor's with Moira on Muir Island. Ye can find him there. And good luck!"

As soon as he'd broken the connection, Banshee turned to find Archangel hovering over his shoulder. "Banshee!" he barked. "Who was that on the comm-link just now? I want a full report immediately. What did you say...*exactly*?"

"Archangel, calm down, lad," Banshee said, taken aback. "It was only Scott and Jean. They were in such a hurry to talk to the professor, they didn't say much of anything. Once I told them he was on Muir Island, they hung right up. They're probably contacting him right now. I'd bet my life on it."

"You shouldn't have done that—relaying that kind of information to unauthorized personnel could put everyone at risk!" Archangel was clearly furious. Banshee could not remember seeing him this angry before.

"Unauthorized personnel? Warren, we're talking about two of yuir very best friends."

"You are right, of course," Archangel said, suddenly calming down. "I'll just phone ahead and alert the professor that they called here. But in the future, Sean, we'd all appreciate it if X-Men communiqués were handled by X-Men. Are we clear on that?"

"Crystal," Banshee said, walking away crushed. He thought of the old Irish proverb: Ye can never go home again. He didn't know if the mansion was "home" anymore.

"Ach, Sean," he scolded himself, "for someone who's built a life on change, ye think ye'd be used to it by now." Disgusted with himself, he went down to the locker room and changed into sweats.

"What I need is a workout in the Danger Room," he said to himself.

But when he got to the Danger Room, he

found that it was occupied—and locked! He activated the computer outside the room, and it flashed to life.

"Remedial program engaged," he read. "Privacy code: No Access. Hmm...Just for the record now, computer, who is currently usin' the Danger Room?"

JUBILEE IS THE LONE OCCUPANT AT THIS TIME, the computer screen read.

"Ach! Now they're allowing minors in solo training sessions?" he said. "I don't want t'be charging in and embarrassin' the child. But I do think this is something I should discuss with the others. Next thing ye know, people'll start traipsing in and out of the professor's Ready Room...?"

His voice trailed off to a whisper as he saw a shadow move down the hall from him. It was Psylocke, emerging from Professor Xavier's Ready Room!

His first instinct was to call out to her, to question what would possibly possess her to enter Professor Xavier's private quarters. Instead, Banshee ducked behind the doorway before she could see him.

He didn't know which was more odd—that

Psylocke would be in the only off-limits room in the entire mansion while the professor was away, or the fact that he'd managed to hide in the shadows from a ninja-trained telepath.

More importantly than that, why did he suddenly get the feeling that if he stepped through the open door to the Ready Room, he might never come out again?

Nevertheless, he went inside. There, he found Gambit and Bishop standing by Cerebro—the computer Professor X had built to detect mutant activity all around the world.

"*Bon soir*, Monsieur Cassidy," Gambit greeted him. "Say hello to the man, Bishop."

"Hello, Sean," Bishop said. "We're a little busy here, making adjustments to Cerebro. Is there anything we can help you with?"

"Not at all," Banshee said. "I just came to look for Charles. Since no one's allowed in here but him, I assumed he'd left the door open."

"Nope," Gambit replied, smiling. "Nobody here but us grunts...doing all de hard work while de professor's on de other side of de pond."

"Since he's started walking again," Banshee

said, returning Gambit's easy grin, "'tis almost impossible to keep track of the man."

"It is not our place to question the professor, Banshee," Bishop said.

"Right ye are about that, Bishop," Banshee replied cheerfully. "He's more'n welcome to come and go as he pleases without reporting to us. Now if you two need a hand, I'll be in—"

Gambit cut him off. "We're fine, *mon ami*."

"Great," Banshee said, already at the door. "I'll catch ye later."

Out in the hallway, he fought down the panic rising inside him. They didn't so much as blink when he lied—saying that the crippled Charles Xavier was walking again. Which meant they were either being mind-controlled...or some shapeshifting invaders had infiltrated mansion security. Either way, Banshee reasoned, this was something Storm should know about immediately.

He ran back to the computer bank next to the Danger Room door. "Computer," he said, "locate Storm, open intra-mansion security channel. Now!"

NONAPPLICABLE. STORM IS NOT CURRENTLY ON THE GROUNDS.

"How is that possible?" he gasped in astonishment. "I just spoke to her ten minutes ago. Computer—locate Archangel."

NONAPPLICABLE. ARCHANGEL IS NOT CURRENTLY ON THE GROUNDS.

"Locate Bishop...Gambit..."

NONAPPLICABLE...

"Computer—identify all essential personnel on grounds at this time!" Banshee ordered frantically. The computer bleeped softly, then the response flashed on the screen.

BANSHEE, ACCESS CORRIDOR 12...WHITE QUEEN, MEDICAL CENTER...JUBILEE, DANGER ROOM...SABRETOOTH, MAXIMUM SECURITY WARD...NO OTHER IDENTIFIABLE LIFE FORMS ON GROUNDS AT THIS TIME.

Banshee gasped in disbelief. "Saints preserve us...!"

Except for himself and Jubilee, all the X-Men had vanished into thin air!

Banshee came to a decision: before he did anything on his own, he would inform Professor
Xavier that something was up. With any luck,
Archangel would have left the Communications Room by now.

He had, but what Archangel had left
behind no longer resembled the Communications Room. The floor panels had been
removed, revealing the thousands of circuit
boards underneath. All the room's sensitive
technology had been laid bare, exposed, and

rewired beyond recognition.

"'Tis nae possible!" Banshee whispered. It would have taken a dozen experts three weeks of working around the clock to totally gut such an elaborate system—and he'd been in here less than half an hour ago!

The way every circuit had been exposed, each wire carefully placed, it was as if the whole room was being...

"Dissected!" he gasped.

The hum of a battery-operated screwdriver caused him to wheel around suddenly. There was Beast—smiling at him from behind a bank of supercomputers.

"I hope that wasn't a very important call you were trying to make, Seanster," the Beast-intruder joked. "I should be done here in about an hour—making adjustments, you know—then it's all yours."

Banshee scratched his head, trying to appear totally relaxed. "'Tis not a problem, lad," he assured Beast's double. "I just wanted t'call Muir Isle and...t'wish Moira a good night."

"Can it wait till morning?" the furry blue creature asked.

Banshee laughed, hoping it didn't sound forced, and backed up toward the doorway. "'Can it wait till morning' to say good night, Hank? Ha! Ye slay me, Henry McCoy—hoo, hoo—ye're always jokin'! But sure'n it can wait. Fact, I'll go set me alarm clock right now! Ha! That is a good one." He turned and left, still laughing.

"Isn't it?" the other said, looking after him, his eyes narrowing.

Shortly afterward, several floors below, Banshee encountered Rogue as he made his way down the main hallway of the maximum security ward. She smiled at him, but her face looked distinctly wary. "Evening, Banshee, sugah," she said.

"Evenin', Rogue," he replied. "'Tis a shame that such a fine lass like yeself is stuck guarding Sabretooth, when ye should be out enjoying a moonlit stroll with Gambit."

Sabretooth had long been one of the X-Men's fiercest enemies. He had razor-sharp claws and teeth and had used them on dozens of his enemies. His berserk rampages had become legend, and the X-Men had traveled the world trying to track him down.

Finally, Sabretooth had walked into the X-Mansion and submitted himself to Professor Xavier's care. He hoped that the professor could cure him of his violent impulses.

For weeks now, he had resided in this tiny cell—for his own protection, and everyone else's. He seemed to be getting better, little by little. Still, he was nowhere near ready to be released.

But now there was no time to waste. Ready or not, Banshee was going to have to set Sabretooth free. This new threat was far more serious—and Banshee was going to need all the help he could get!

Rogue crossed her arms and leaned back against the door of Sabretooth's cell. Clearly, she wasn't going anywhere.

"Ah don't mind it—being alone, that is," she told him. "Ah'm supposed to be alone down here." She looked at him pointedly. "With nobody else around."

"I'll be out of yuir way in a minute," he assured her. "I'm just here t'take Sabretooth for his daily walk." Giving her a smile, he rapped three times on the door of the cell.

"Ah've already taken him outside today,"

Rogue said. "In fact, we just got back."

When Banshee ignored her, the smile left her face. "Banshee? Ah said Ah've already attended to the man's needs. There is no reason for you to open his cell at this time."

She grabbed his wrist as he reached for the red button that unlocked the cell door and deactivated the force field that kept Sabretooth from escaping. "Banshee? Are you listening to me?"

"That I am, darling," he replied. "Now ye listen to me!" Yanking his wrist free suddenly, he stepped back and opened his mouth wide. From the depths of his being, a sound emerged—a sound unlike any other on the planet.

Banshee's sonic scream—his mutant power, his birthright—was capable of splitting steel with the precision of a laser beam or leveling small mountains.

It shredded the techno-organic living circuitry of the Phalanx unit that, a moment ago, had looked exactly like Rogue!

"On me sainted mother's grave...!" Banshee gasped as the Rogue clone popped, sizzled, and disintegrated. "'Tis one o' the creatures Gambit

battled last week in New York City!"

Gambit had told the other X-Men about his recent encounter with the strange beings—Phalanx, he'd called them—but now, it appeared, they'd taken over the X-Mansion entirely!

But were these creatures only replicas of the team? Banshee wondered. Or had the Phalanx actually assimilated the X-Men?

"On yuir feet, man!" he ordered the muscular mutant who lay on the cell floor. Creed's hands and mouth were encased in adamantium restraints. Underneath, Banshee knew, were the rippling muscles, the fangs and claws...

"The mansion's security has been compromised," he told Creed, "leaving ye, me, Jubilee, and the White Queen knee-deep in Phalanx!"

"Was countin' on one o' ya piecin' things t'gether," Sabretooth said, coming awake. "Just didn't think it'd be you, Irish."

Creed was on his feet now, and seemed to be recovering quickly. "So," he growled. "Ya got a game plan?"

His answer came, not from Banshee, but

from the Phalanx unit that had been Rogue's clone. Now, having pulled itself back together, it suddenly blocked the doorway of the cell!

"As carbonites—especially as mutagenic variables—your fate is termination!"

The techno-organic monster continued to speak even as Sabretooth came flying at it with a powerful body slam.

"If the collective intelligence was not otherwise engaged in deciphering vital information we have gathered here, it would authorize us to—"

"Yeah, yeah, yeah," Sabretooth said, delivering blow after blow to the thing's humanlike head.

"Shoulda, coulda, woulda!" Sabretooth mocked. "Ya done a good job o' discombobulatin' her, Banshee—but nothin' short of obliterating 'em is enough to stop these jokers. Sit back, Irish. And take notes."

It had been weeks since Sabretooth had been able to cut loose. As Professor Xavier's patient, Creed had been undergoing psionic therapy in order to control his bestial nature—and to subdue his frenzied rages. He had been showing progress, too—until now.

The animal had been let out of its cage—and he wouldn't have it any other way. Surveying the techno-organic debris scattered around the room, he smiled.

"That was fun," he said. "Now give me one reason I shouldn't give you some of the same."

"Because," Banshee replied evenly, "the detonator in my hand is hooked to yuir muzzle, Creed. One wrong move, and ye join yuir friend here on the far corner o' the floor."

"Hmmm...just asking," Sabretooth said. "Again, what's the plan?"

"Ye free Jubilee and the White Queen," Banshee said gravely, "and *I'll* see about the exterminating..."

"Situation: Phalanx/Rogue has ceased transmission." The Phalanx unit impersonating Bishop turned to the Gambit unit in alarm. "Analysis: designate Banshee has been alerted to our presence."

"Save the techno-speak for the mainframe, *'mon ami,'*" the Gambit unit replied. The circuits of his arm were organically connected to those of the exposed computer bank.

"It doesn't matter how much Banshee

knows. Once we've downloaded all of Xavier's files—and analyzed the Cerebro mutant detection program, utilizing the X-Men captives as test subjects—the Phalanx will finally be able to assimilate mutants just as easily as we do humans."

Suddenly, two shots from a blaster exploded the circuitry, shattering the Phalanx units.

"Exactly what I wanted to hear, lad," Banshee said, firing the blaster again. "Because that means the X-Men are still alive—an' all we have to do is find them!"

He finished off the two units with several more blasts. "Pardon the use of a firearm," he said, "but I know from what the others told me that ye possess the ability to adapt t'whatever mutant powers are used against ye—an' I felt it was time to be creative."

The room was quiet, except for the sizzle of short-circuiting equipment. "All I need to do now," he told himself, "is t'set the self-destruct sequence and blow the Ready Room. I'm praying the other three are farin' as well up above."

The Storm unit felt herself disintegrating. "Warning: encephalon pattern disruption," she called out to the Iceman unit. "Unit frame endo-skeletal dispersion: imminent!"

"It is as if my mmmind..." the Iceman unit groaned, "werrrre tearrringgg...itttssssellfff appparrrrttt!"

"That's a pretty good description of what I just did to you," said Emma Frost to the disintegrating units as she pointed her hands toward them. "And it's certainly no worse than what you planned for me, had Mr. Creed not released me."

Sabretooth appeared in the doorway behind her, holding Jubilee, unconscious, in one massive arm. "Sorry I took so long, Frost," he said. "Had t'pluck pint-size here out of the Danger Room on my way. I'd hate for Jubilee to die before I had a chance to settle with her—"

"You're boring me, Creed," the White Queen told him, her ice-blue eyes flashing. "Let us continue ridding this place of—"

"Uh-uh, lady," he cut her off. "Banshee wants a rendezvous downside—now!"

"What possible interest would I have in what Banshee wants?" she challenged him, brushing her long blond hair away from her face with a flick of her wrist.

"We're not talking about your interests, frail," he told her, grabbing her hand in his iron grip and dragging her along with him. "We're talkin' about mine! 'Sides, as impressive as your psi-bolt was, the same trick don't work twice on the Phalanx!"

"How can I be certain I can trust you, Sabretooth?" she asked as she ran at his side, trying to keep up with him.

"Trust me?" he repeated, never breaking stride. "Ha! That's a hoot."

Alone in the Ready Room—knowing he wouldn't be alone for long—Banshee read the monitor. "SELF-DESTRUCT ENGAGED: 2 MINUTES..." A mechanical voice echoed the words aloud.

"Cerebro?" Banshee asked quickly. "Show me—exactly—what program was running a moment ago."

Cerebro obliged him, a screen full of data coming up on his right.

"Neogenetic manifestation," he read. "Bio-signature: File 72234: Monet St. Croix... Everett Thomas...Angelo Espinosa...Clarice Ferguson..."

"Ninety seconds..." the mechanical voice droned.

"Sweet saints!" Banshee breathed. "Charles's list of the next generation of mutants—they're goin' after the children!"

"Seventy-five..."

"Cerebro," he commanded, "display neo-genetic geomatrix." Instantly, a map of the world pinpointing several locations came on the view screen.

"Did those creatures manage to download this information?" Banshee wondered. "Does the Phalanx know where these mutants are?"

"Sixty seconds..."

Banshee heard the warning, but he still had business to take care of. Using Cerebro's alternate circuits, he flashed a brief message to Xavier on Muir Island. UNDER ATTACK BY PHALANX! X-MEN MISSING! SEND HELP AT ONCE!

"Cerebro!" he ordered frantically. "Print out a copy of the map!"

"Thirty seconds..." came the reply as the map fed out into Banshee's hands.

His work done, Banshee turned to go. But before he could make a move, the doorway was blocked by three Phalanx units! Banshee recognized his attackers as Beast, Psylocke, and Archangel.

The Archangel unit spoke first. But the others joined in. Banshee could see now that all three Phalanx units were really part of one huge being—what they called their "core consciousness."

"The welfare of the next generation of mutants is not your concern! They are but genetic raw material for our techno-organic core. Or they will be, once they are assimilated by the Phalanx. Until then the only way to deal with unruly mutants...is to eliminate them!"

Banshee smiled back at them, listening as the mechanical voice of Cerebro counted down the final seconds.

"Well, that was honest of ye," he told the Phalanx cheerfully. "So I'll be equally honest when I say...later!"

"Escape from the Phalanx is impos—"

Kaboom!

In the instant before the explosion destroyed the Phalanx units, Banshee looked down at the floor and let out a sonic scream. The scream sent waves downward, blasting a hole in the floor. He jumped down, still screaming, the sonic waves clearing a path through the solid brick and steel in front of him.

He only hoped Professor Xavier would forgive him. They'd lost a lifetime of information stored inside Cerebro's memory banks. But there had been no other way.

He landed softly on all fours, thanks to cushioning sound waves, and found himself in the storm drains below the mansion. There, in the wet darkness, Sabretooth and the others were waiting for him. "What took you so long, Mr. Cassidy?" Emma Frost demanded.

"Cut Irish some slack, Frost," Sabretooth told her. "He was probably trackin' down the rest of the X-Sheep."

"Not far off, Creed," Banshee said as they helped him to his feet. "I managed t'dispatch a message to Xavier, explaining what happened. He knows that he and Excalibur have to track down the X-Men." Looking down at the still-unconscious Jubilee, he asked, "Is she all right?"

"She's fine," Emma Frost snapped. "Now why aren't *we* searching for the X-Men?"

"Because those creatures had access to a file filled with new, untrained young mutants," Banshee answered. "Men and women we might have contacted eventually. Innocents who know nothing o' this."

He stared off into the distance. "They are the next generation of mutants," he said solemnly. "Our future. We have to find them—before the Phalanx does!"

Monaco, a tiny country on the south coast of France, has long been the home of some of the world's wealthiest people. On a mountainous road, high above the country's capital, a beautiful, dark-skinned young woman rode in the back seat of her limousine. Beside her sat her chaperone, a large woman who was also her bodyguard.

"'I don't care how much money you're paying me,' I says to him," the woman was saying in a Cockney accent. "'You're off your blooming chop, you are!'

"I ask you," she said, turning to the girl, who sat staring blankly out the window at the dark, wet night. The window was partly open, and the girl's face and hair were soaking wet.

"What could that father of yours be thinking?" the woman wondered. "It's been three months since you've said a single word to anyone. Day or night—it makes no difference to you, does it? You just sit there in your own world. Mercy, m'dear—you don't even know enough to come in out of the rain. Monet? Monet?" The woman sighed in exasperation.

The girl's green eyes continued to stare blankly. The raindrops, like tears, trickled down her light brown cheeks.

"I understand your father is upset," the woman went on, carrying on the one-way conversation. "Especially after what happened to the twins and your brother...but he simply cannot go on pretending you don't need help. I even suggested the United States. 'There's a chap named Xavier,' I told him, 'has an exclusive school there for what he calls gifted youngsters.'

"All it would take is one word from you, Monet, and I'm sure your father would at least consider it. Trust Missus Gayle—something has to give soon..."

Something did. Suddenly, the limousine's entire electrical system went haywire!

The two-million-dollar automobile had been designed to withstand an assault by an army of terrorists. But all of its armor was absolutely useless against the Phalanx.

"Communication, core central: Contact established. Encounter with mutant designate—target: imminent. Vehicle driver—non-essential—will be absorbed."

An immense techno-organic hand closed over the injured driver's face. Microcircuits began growing underneath his skin almost instantly.

"Absorbing genetic refuse for future trans-mode assimilation," the Phalanx unit told core central.

For the first time in her entire life, retired Lieutenant Colonel Gayle Cord-Becker, former director of MI-6, one of Britain's intelligence agencies, was left speechless. "My God..." was all she could say.

The Phalanx unit, having finished with the driver, pressed its face against the partition separating the front and back seats. "Biocentric analysis: human, post-prime. Conclusion: not a threat."

"So you say!" she cried, shoving the far door open and pushing Monet out of the vehicle. "Go, child! Run, and don't look back! Once they notice we're missing, your father's people will come looking. Now quit staring, girl...and *move it!*"

"Superfluous behavior. It is impossible to escape the Phalanx!" The Phalanx unit smashed the window and ripped out the car door, reaching for the older woman.

But Gayle Cord-Becker was not through yet. "Who said anything about escape, luv?" she said. "Now come to Colonel Cord-Becker, you heartless creature—because I'm going to send you back to whatever factory spawned you!"

Gayle Cord-Becker's courage was valiant, but ineffective against the Phalanx. The bodyguard's scream echoed in the night as the Phalanx unit absorbed her.

Monet St. Croix stared blankly at it all, sitting on the side of the road in the pouring rain. She remained motionless, even as the huge Phalanx unit rose and approached her.

"Automobile: absorbed. Carbonites: assimilated. Designate: Monet St. Croix, within range. Biocentric analysis: b-bi-bio...cennntri-iicc annnn—"

The beast, its snarling face only inches from Monet's, glared at her. "Unable to execute biocentric scan at this time due to intense level of psionic interference. Evidence supports collective intelligence's theory. Quarry may be most powerful of the next generation of *Homo superior*. That is why she is scheduled for termination!"

Large techno-organic tentacles enveloped her. "Note: Subject does not respond to violence or threats of death. Subject responds to no outside stimuli."

The Phalanx unit enclosed Monet completely. The techno-organic mass lost its shape, slowly turning into a glowing oval of circuitry. "First 'Generation Next' mutant successfully apprehended. Uploading transmode sequence. Destination: way station, to await final compilation of mutagenetic testing data."

The glowing oval disappeared, taking Monet St. Croix with it.

A cool breeze blew along the hillsides overlooking the Guthrie family farm in Cumberland County, Kentucky. It was a quiet night.

"Paige!" The scream had come from her mother's bedroom. Paige Guthrie ran upstairs and threw open the door, only to find her mother being enveloped by the tentacles of some hideous monster. It had a human face, but the body looked like a computer's interior!

She knew at once what it was—her older brother Sam, otherwise known as X-Force's superpowered Cannonball, had phoned her a few days ago from Europe to warn her about the Phalanx.

"*Paige!* Oh, Lord—stay back!" her mother screamed as Paige, blond hair streaming in all directions, grabbed her mother's arm and pulled her away from the creature.

"*No!* Ah'm not gonna let you go, Momma! Ah'm *not!*"

Paige's brothers and sisters ran into the room and looked on in horror.

"J-Joshua—w-what is that?"

"Ah dunno, 'Lisabeth! But all o' you stay away! If Ah could only get t'the barn an' get out Daddy's old pitchfork—but we don' even have time for that!" He grabbed Paige around her waist, to keep her from being sucked into the monster's grasp. "Paige, you hang on, hear, girl?"

"Ah'm tryin', Josh!" she cried. "My arm hurts so much!"

"Paige!" her mother screamed. "For pity's sake, girl—let go of me! Both of you—get the children out of here!"

"That would be an admirable sacrifice on your part, human," a chilling, half-mechanical voice emanating from the monster said. "Would that we were truly interested in assimilating you to begin with. The truth is, we merely sought to use you as bait—to lure in the Generation Next mutant!"

"Mutant—?" the mother gasped. "Oh, Lord—*No!* You're after Paige?"

Her son Sam had already left home because he had mutant abilities and wanted to use them to help the world. He was now a member of X-Force, one of Professor Xavier's mutant teams. Mrs. Guthrie had always known Paige would leave one day, too. But she'd never imagined it would be like this.

"Target designate: Guthrie, Paige. Mutagenetic abilities: transitional body-morph. Target: acquired," the unit said as it let go of Mrs. Guthrie and grabbed Paige instead. "Target assimilation: impeded, as expected. Proceed with retrieval."

"Momma! It's got Paige now!" Joshua yelled. "Use your powers, Paige! Do something!"

But it was too late. The huge monster

exploded upward, taking the roof of their house along with it.

"You know she can't just change at will, Josh," Mrs. Guthrie reminded her son. Paige still needed to learn how to master her abilities.

The creature that captured Paige flew upward into the moonlit sky. "Target successfully retrieved and removed from premises." A moment later, it disappeared.

The Guthrie family looked up at the stars, stunned and grieving.

"Paige...my baby..." her mother moaned softly.

"What can we do, Momma?" Jeb, her middle son, asked.

"Ah don't know, Jeb," she said. "May the Lord have mercy on us...Ah don't know. 'Cause I get the strong feelin' that not even your brother Sam, or Charles Xavier an' his X-Men, can save your sister now."

She awoke—if you could call it that—to find them crawling all over her like worms made of hot wire. They burrowed under her eyelids, searching, probing...

Monet didn't scream. She could hear them talking as she hung there, suspended by the tendrils which worked their way slowly into her being.

Their mechanical chatter buzzed in her head. They called themselves the Phalanx. Their goal, as far as she could tell, was to assimilate all life on Earth into their living techno-organic collective intelligence. For everyone to see with their eyes, hear with their ears, speak with their voice, think with one mind...

The Phalanx tried and failed to assimilate Monet St. Croix. But what they did not realize was that she was learning as much about them as they were about her!

She noted that there were several of them in the room. But two seemed to be of greater importance than the others—the ones called Lang and Hodge. The Lang unit seemed more human than the others. Monet wondered if that meant anything.

"Biocentric analysis: subject: mutant life-form: Monet St. Croix—assimilation unsux-sux-successful."

"Query: is subject designate status as a mutant carbonite solely responsible for absorption failure?"

"78-33-processing-22001 affirmative..."

"Confirmed. Mutants still remain beyond the grasp of Phalanx absorption. They are—as always—a mystery."

The one they called Hodge now spoke.

"But why do only mutants resist assimilation to the collective?"

"They are a different life form from humans," the one called Lang responded. "But that is something we have always known, isn't it, Hodge?"

"Affirmative, Lang. And we have both failed in our attempts to assimilate them. It is for this reason that the collective seeks to eliminate all mutant interference. And that is precisely why the next generation of Xavier's brood must be found!"

"And if these children cannot be assimilated?" the Lang unit asked.

"Then they—like all who op-op-oppose the Phalanx—must be destroyed!"

Hodge's response frightened Lang, although he didn't dare to show it.

As humans, both he and Hodge had been bitter enemies of mutantkind. So great was their hatred that both, along with many others since, had given themselves up to the Phalanx. They had agreed to be assimilated. Techno-organic circuits had taken over their bodies and their minds.

They were now part of the collective intelligence. They had given up their humanity so they could join the fight to destroy mutants everywhere. Both had been picked to lead the Earth invasion force.

Lang had been given a special job. He had been left partly human so that he could be the link between the Phalanx's central core and humankind.

Together, he and Hodge had helped create the collective intelligence to get to their goal of destroying mutantkind.

But now, Lang found himself holding back. Hodge's words had frozen his still-human blood. He quietly put up walls inside his own mind—walls he could hide behind, where he could think thoughts that were sheltered from Hodge and the others.

Lang was beginning to realize that something was wrong. The Phalanx were evolving beyond his expectations—beyond human control. They were now seeing the world in ways which, he feared, could pose even more trouble for humankind than it did for mutants.

Had Lang allied with a monster he couldn't control? To end the mutant species he hated so much, had he endangered all of humanity as well?

"You gentlemen have got to be kidding me." Sixteen-year-old Everett Thomas stood on the steps of the precinct house. He stared down at an entire squadron of police officers, all with their guns pointed straight at him.

Everett folded his hands on his chest. He wore high-top sneakers and a baseball cap, and looked like a typical teenager. But Everett Thomas was nothing of the kind.

"Do you intend to arrest me simply because I yelled too loud?" he asked the officers.

"No, Thomas," one of the policemen replied. "It's because when you shouted, every single window between Gravols and Grand was blown out!"

"That's reckless endangerment," added another officer, "vandalism, maybe even negligent assault tacked on! So what was that all about, kid?"

The police were frightened. They had always known Everett Thomas as a good kid—a straight-A student, the whole works. But then things had started happening—odd things—and all they knew was that Everett always seemed to be at the center of them.

They didn't know he was a mutant—that he had the power to temporarily get "in sync" with any mutant power he came in contact with. Everett himself barely knew about his powers. He only knew he was different. And what was more, he enjoyed it. But at this moment, the only thing the police understood was that he might be very dangerous.

"Officers, relax!" he said. "As I tried to explain earlier, the windows were only an aftereffect! I had my hands kind of full at the time!"

"So you said, kid," one of the officers broke in skeptically. "Some sort of creatures made out of liquid metal...like we're supposed to believe that!"

"I think it's a safe bet that at least half of you believe me," Everett replied with an ironic smile, looking at the microcircuits suddenly glowing under the skin of some of the officers.

"What're you talking about...?" The officer's words trailed off as he turned to see the Phalanx units. They were now transforming into their hideous natural form.

"Target designate: Everett Thomas—proceed with assimilation initiative."

"Target acquired: Thomas, Everett—mutagenic abilities: unspecified—proceed with caution."

"I've got a better idea," Everett replied as one of them reached out a tentacle that quickly turned into a giant clawed hand, which grabbed for his throat. "Don't proceed at all!

"These are the things I was telling you about, officers," he managed to say as the claws closed over his trachea. "Now do you believe me?"

Skreeeeeeeeshaaaaaa!

The monstrous claw let go at the earsplitting sound of the sonic scream. Everett gasped for breath. "What now?" he wondered.

"Structure under assault from a previously registered mutagenetic signature: sonic assault, multi-decibel level. Structure cannot maintain..."

The police were running for their lives. *"Move! Move!"* their captain was shouting.

"Do you hear that?" a sergeant asked, as the deafening screams continued. "That sound—it's earpiercing!"

"Well," Everett said, recovering his breath and managing a satisfied grin at the smashed Phalanx units lying on the ground. "That would explain my trick with the windows earlier, wouldn't it? I must have gotten in sync with someone in the area who had superpowers, and that means the cavalry has arrived!"

At that moment, the screamer came flying onto the scene, wearing some sort of uniform that Everett had never seen. Another figure with tigerlike claws and a metal mask came up behind him!

"Let's hit 'em hard, Irish!" the tiger-man was saying. "Let's have some fun!"

In the few seconds Everett had taken to catch his breath, the Phalanx had also recovered. Somehow, they managed to re-form from the rubble of microcircuitry the scream had blasted them into.

"Establishing contact with the collective regarding the advised next step."

But Everett was gazing at his rescuers. "Would you look at them?" he said admiringly, even as the Phalanx came at him again.

"Sabretooth—the lad—get him!" the uniformed one ordered before launching another incredible scream.

The one called Sabretooth lashed out, slamming into the attackers. Techno-organic tentacles flew in all directions.

"Disfun-funkk-function—regisregis—tered in appendage molecules. Mutant designate: Banshee [subdesignate: Cassidy, Sean], ability to control vocal pitch to the point of modulating and casting decibel-variant sonic calls."

Sabretooth took Everett in his arms and ran from the wounded attackers. "In other words, you idiots," he called back at them, "he yells real loud! I got the kid, Cassidy. We're clear— so cut loose!"

Banshee's next scream was deafening. It was so intense that it liquefied the techno-organic beings.

"I always thought you had it in you, Irish," Sabretooth shouted. "Nice t'see it come out!"

"Wow," was all the astonished Everett could manage to say.

"Stop shouting, Creed, I'm finished," Banshee said, folding his arms on his chest as the police began to straggle back onto the scene.

"A mutant, you said?" one asked the captain. "Should we arrest him?"

"What for?" the captain asked. "For saving our lives? I don't think so."

"Officers, your thanks are enough," Banshee told them. "Now, Creed, what were ye bellowin' about, man?"

"It was interestin' t'see a darker side o' you, Irish," Sabretooth replied. "A little bit o' me."

"Aye, not as much as ye'd like t'see, boyo, perhaps," Banshee said. "But more'n enough for me, I assure ye."

"Not to sound ungrateful or anything," Everett broke in, "but can someone explain to me exactly what's going on?"

"That we will, Everett, lad," Banshee said, "as soon as we get out of here."

"But my family—"

"They'll be fine, son," Banshee told him. "It's only mutants these Phalanx are after. Specifically, *new* mutants. And that, me friend, means *you*."

⊗ ⊗ ⊗ **6** ⊗ ⊗ ⊗

On a busy nearby street corner, Emma Frost and Jubilee stood waiting for Banshee and Sabretooth to return with the young mutant they'd gone to rescue. Jubilee was standing on the hood of their car, scanning the street, while the White Queen had her hands to her temples and her eyes closed.

"You hear anything on the ol' telepathic intercom, Frost?" Jubilee asked her.

"They've found and rescued the boy, Everett Thomas," Emma answered, "and are returning here. By the way, Jubilee," she added, opening her eyes, "get off the car. Now. A little less drawing of attention seems advisable."

"Listen, Ms. Frost," Jubilee shot back, blowing a gigantic bubble with the wad of gum in her mouth, "just 'cause yer bummed about what happened t'your ol' students, the Hellions, doesn't mean that us young mutants shouldn't be seen or heard. Keepin' us all hidden an' ignorant 'bout what's goin' down in the world isn't gonna keep us safe, y'know."

Being treated like a kid always made Jubilee mad, and now that Emma Frost had done it, she was determined to have her say. But now she realized that even though she was talking loudly and standing on the car's hood, no one in the street seemed to notice her.

"Hey," she asked, "what's with the straight genes?"

"You wonder why the humans walk by us without a second glance?" the White Queen inquired. "Simple. I am telepathically masking our presence from them. The less obtrusive we remain, the better for us. And it is a task made much easier for me, girl, if you would kindly keep *quiet!*"

Jubilee frowned and winced. "Yeah, sure thing, Ms. Emma Frost, used ta be the mucki-ty-muck White Queen of the Inner Circle," she mumbled to herself as she got down off the car. "'Fore the X-Men whupped you every time out...then the Sentinels fried yer brains, an' you ended up wakin' up a year later—an' now we're stuck with you an' Sabretooth out here in St. Louis—*shooor* I'll keep quiet, that's me. Li'l Miss Obtrusive—not..."

She blew another bubble, tapping her foot anxiously on the pavement. "I'm not nervous, not at all," she continued to mutter under her breath. "But I do wish Wolveroonie were here...he'd wipe out these walking Slinkies for shoor...then wipe the floor with *you* just for fun—you'd see! Hmm?"

The bubble popped all over Jubilee's face as she looked up to see several Phalanx units hovering over her, tentacles raised.

"Uhm, Mth. Frotht, ma'am, lady...um..." she stammered, her mouth still full of bubble gum. "I dink we're in trubble..."

It took a quick leap for both of them to avoid the grabbing tentacles. "Hey, Frosty," she shouted as they landed in the clear, "what're we gonna do now?"

"Well, child," the White Queen replied, "since my telepathic abilities don't have any power over these creatures as they did at Xavier's—and you, obviously, are still a novice despite your bravado—I would say that we're going to *die!*"

"Hmm," Jubilee said with a smirk as a Phalanx unit reached for her. "Good plan...no wonder yer Hellions're toast!"

"Target assimilation is an ineligible action. Proceed to eliminate Frost, Emma, in order to facilitate retrieval of Generation Next target: Lee, Jubilation."

"Stay behind me, girl," the White Queen instructed her, "and close your eyes."

But just as Jubilee was about to obey, a sonic scream split the night. When she opened her eyes again, the Phalanx units had shattered.

"Gross!" she said with a grimace. "Uhm, what happened?"

"Looks like these clowns can't compensate fer Irish's powers," Sabretooth explained as he, Banshee, and Everett appeared on the scene.

"Long as he changes the frequency o' his sonic scream!"

"Sqqchik chik chik...It is only a matter of time...Creed, Victor, shikkzz shik before designate: Banshee's wavelength spectrum has been analyzed and compensated for."

"Big deal!" Sabretooth roared back at the Phalanx unit, which had already reconstructed itself from its own wreckage. "You'll still have me to deal with! Try t'compensate fer *that!*"

"Sabretooth puts on a brave front," Emma Frost told Jubilee as they watched Sabretooth attack. "But he knows full well the true measure of his opponents. It is only a matter of time before we're overwhelmed."

Suddenly, she reached out and grabbed Jubilee by her hair. "Come here, Jubilation," she ordered. With her other hand, the White Queen took Everett by the arm.

"Hey—" Jubilee complained. "What're you—"

"Everett, open your mind to mine," the White Queen said, ignoring Jubilee. "If you wish to survive this night, do not resist me now, for this may be our last hope of escaping! I am going to link our three minds..."

"Solution found to designate: Banshee's sonic cries. To prevent his shouts, place techno-organic matter inside his throat cavity."

It was no sooner said than done. Banshee was incapacitated as a techno-organic tentacle reached around his neck and covered his mouth, trying to force its way inside.

"If Banshee is to live," Emma Frost told Everett, "I must become a telepathic conduit between you and Jubilee. If I understand your mutant abilities correctly, Everett, you must see Jubilee through my eyes to access her pyrokinetic abilities with your own powers— and use her mutant gift in ways she has been afraid to! In short, by detonating the very matter with which these techno-organic beings are composed of on a subatomic level!"

Kraka-booom!

The explosion created by Everett Thomas, as he hooked his powers up with Jubilee, made the sonic wail of Banshee seem like a whisper.

The dust settled...the X-Men had survived. The Phalanx—at least for now—had not.

"Did I just do that?" Jubilee asked in a nervous, high-pitched voice.

"No," Everett breathed. "I did."

"Even better," Jubilee said, relieved.

"We don't have much time, Cassidy," Emma Frost said as she helped him to his feet. "Eventually, their collective intelligence will reconfigure the techno-organic matter into a new Phalanx."

"Eventually, Frost?" Banshee replied, looking upward.

Emma Frost turned and gasped, as the ooze formed itself up into a mountainous Phalanx unit!

"Of course...for we of the Phalanx can be anywhere—anytime. You performed impressively here, but in the overall scheme of things, X-Men, this is a minor victory at best."

Banshee gazed up at the Phalanx unit in amazement—it spoke in plain English, unlike the other units he'd encountered. And now that he looked at it, it had a familiar face!

"Lang?" Banshee cried in astonishment. "*You're* involved in this? Ye *are* Stephen Lang— the madman who tried t'kill the X-Men years ago with a Sentinel attack—inside o' all that rubbish, aren't ye?"

"In a manner of speaking, Cassidy.

Actually, I am projecting my consciousness through the techno-organic mesh. But that is unimportant. What does matter, however, is that you recognize the fact that resistance is truly futile. You see, X-Men, this day of triumph over your kind has been in preparation for a long time."

The Lang projection towered over them, as real-looking as any other Phalanx unit, but apparently unable to act against them as the others had.

"In many ways, we've had the help of those who knew you best: Cameron Hodge...Archangel's beloved girlfriend Candy Southern...Jean Grey's long-lost sister Sara... she was a difficult one. Her mental strength is truly remarkable—much like her sister's. But in the end, she, too, surrendered.

"We know you, X-Men. We own you, inside and out! For, you see, the Phalanx rose from the ashes of two things which you're very familiar with. The techno-organic remains of your deceased comrade, Warlock— and my own burning, breathing, living hatred for your entire pathetic species!"

"Lang, listen to me," Emma Frost called

out. "You have to see through your idiotic prejudice and acknowledge that the Phalanx have grown far beyond your ability to control them! You're playing with fire, Lang! These are no longer simply fanatics who have accepted the transmode virus and given up their humanity to become your techno-organic servants—they're something more!"

"What I have done, Frost, is create something that allows humans to climb one rung higher than mutants on the evolutionary ladder to defend themselves! Through the Phalanx, mankind will finally be able to rid itself of the mutant threat. And with every moment you waste, another step is taken toward accomplishing that goal!"

With a hideous laugh, the Lang creature lifted a human face from the ooze—a face Emma Frost knew too well...

"Recognize this child? While you were fighting to save Everett Thomas, Paige Guthrie has been taken! And so, another of your precious next generation of mutants falls to the onslaught of the Phalanx! I will see you broken, mutants, in spirit as well as body—the Age of Humanity is assured!"

"And what have you unleashed on this world in order for that to happen, Lang?" the White Queen challenged him. "Go! Continue to delude yourself into thinking that the Phalanx are merely a means to eradicate mutation from the Earth. Don't you realize you're in danger of sacrificing the very humanity you seek so desperately to protect?"

But the image of Lang was fading. Having delivered its message, it sank back into the ooze.

"Hate never stops to reason, Emma," Banshee said. "You, more'n anyone, should know that! But he has another one o' the kids, blast his hide!"

"We have one advantage Lang isn't aware of, Cassidy," Emma said. "When he showed us the Guthrie girl, I was able to make telepathic contact with her psychic imprint."

"You're sayin' ye can track the lass down?" he asked hopefully.

"Would that I could," she replied. "The contact was fleeting, at best. I can pinpoint a general location."

"It'll have t' do, then," he said. "Let's find out how many more from the list they've taken—an' then raid their stronghold t'save those poor souls."

"Guys! Guys!" Jubilee interrupted them urgently. "Listen to me! Haven't ya noticed someone's been kinda conspicuously absent by his silence...not to mention his charming personality?"

"What—" Banshee looked at his wrist. The detonator—the one that had the ability to explode the adamantium muzzle—had been damaged during the fight!

"Oh, no..." he whispered, glancing around and seeing the broken restraints lying on the ground. "He knew it! Blast him—he did it! As if things aren't bad enough, Sabretooth has escaped!"

7

Paige Guthrie returned to consciousness slowly, her vision still blurred. She was in a bluish, bubblelike room. The walls were strange, too. They were constructed from throbbing microcircuits and seemed almost alive. Patches of wall glowed, providing dim light.

She rubbed the back of her neck, remembering what had happened to her.

Like most teenagers, Paige believed she'd seen it all. But after being kidnapped from her family's farmhouse in Kentucky, and taken to this unknown place, she wasn't sure she knew anything anymore.

It felt as if someone had been using the back of her neck as a pincushion. On the other hand, the pain was proof that she was still alive—and for that, she was grateful.

She lifted the blanket off her legs...blanket? *How weird,* she thought—that the Phalanx would be rude enough to kidnap her under the threat of death, but polite enough to cover her with a blanket.

But it wasn't a blanket at all. It was the distended skin of a mutant boy! He looked at her, scowling, his skin wrapped over him like a loose-fitting cloak, all in folds.

Most teenagers would have been shocked by this. But as the younger sister of X-Force's Cannonball, Paige already thought of herself as sort of an X-Man. So she managed to stay calm and collected. "Um, hello," she said.

"Buenos días, chica," the boy answered glumly. "Welcome to the worst place on earth."

"Gosh, Angelo! There's no reason to be so depressing." The voice belonged to a handsome, muscular boy with blond hair and high cheekbones. "They are frightened enough as it is without you being so...so negative."

They? Yes, there were two other females in the room, Paige saw now. Both wearing skintight dark blue outfits like hers.

One, a gorgeous dark-skinned girl, sat against the far wall, staring into space as if the rest of them didn't exist. The other, who had spiked hair and dark purple circles around her eyes, was huddled timidly in the blond's arms, shivering with fear.

"Excuse me, Gregor," the boy called Angelo answered. "But I was only trying to be realistic. Someone—or ones—went to a lot of trouble to kidnap the five of us. I doubt we're here for a festival."

"Those someones are called the Phalanx," Paige told them, as she got up and scoped out the walls of the room. But not really a room. The walls seemed to be techno-organic—half-flesh, half-microcircuitry.

"They're an alien race with no great love of mutants," she went on. "Which is what Ah am, and what Ah am assuming we all are. But don't panic! I'll get us out o' here and we'll contact people who can help us—people called the X-Men. They're a team of mutants who protect the world against just such a threat as the Phalanx."

There was a long silence. Then Angelo spoke up. "Wow," he said. "Good thing the country mouse showed up to save the day. What did you think, we've been sitting here on our butts waiting for you to wake up and rescue us? It ain't going to happen. We've tried everything to get out of here."

"My apologies, Mr. Competent," Paige replied, a little annoyed. "I saw you in a heap and your friend here was in a catatonic stupor, so I automatically assumed you could use help."

"There, there, boys and girls," the handsome guy called Gregor interrupted, smiling. "Let's not argue among ourselves. I betcha if we all pitch in and work together, we'll all be home for dinner."

"Yeah...and we can put on a show in the barn while we're at it, too," Paige said sarcastically. "Angelo, is he always like this?"

"He has been since I've been here," Angelo replied.

Suddenly, the shivering girl in Gregor's

arms spoke up, her voice a mere whisper as a tear made its way down her cheek. "It doesn't matter what we try," she said. "We're all going to die."

"My name is Paige, darlin'. You are…?"

"Clarice."

"Listen to me, Clarice," Paige said, kneeling down in front of her, "Everything is goin' t'be fine. I have certain friends who are looking for me right now. Friends who won't stop for nothing—for anything—until I'm free. When that happens, we're all walking out of here together. Until then, I need you to be strong for me…for all of us. Can you do that, Clarice?"

Paige held up Clarice's chin, and the weeping girl nodded. "I can try…not to cry," she said, wiping the tears from her huge blue eyes.

"We've established that you make very nice speeches, Paige," Angelo said dryly. "Now when they return to experiment on one of us again, perhaps you can bore them into submission."

Paige ignored him and focused on Clarice, who was looking back at her strangely. "Paige," she said softly. "Please, tell me, I really need to know..."

"Anything, Clarice. What is it?"

"Will your friends be here...before you disappear?"

"Whu—?" Paige followed Clarice's gaze down to her own midsection. There, on her stomach, was a growing techno-organic mass!

"The transmode virus!" Paige gasped in horror, recognizing it from what her brother Sam had told her about the alien beings. It was the way the Phalanx took over human bodies—but she was not human, she was a mutant!

"Ah must have been infected when Ah was attacked by one of them. He called himself Harvest!" she said, remembering vividly the Phalanx unit with the bearded face and body armor who had brought her to this place after she was kidnapped. "And...the infection's spreadin'!"

Paige fought down the panic that was rising inside her. "Nothin' to worry about," she whispered to herself. "I'm sure the X-Men will be here in plenty of time."

But she wasn't sure. She wasn't sure at all.

"Jeepers," Gregor said, stroking his chin

thoughtfully. "It looks like the Phalanx managed to do to you what it couldn't do to the rest of us. As near as we can tell, they can't— what was that word—'assimilate' mutants the way they do humans. It's the whole reason we've been brought here. We're sort of test subjects, so they can perfect the technique on us. Before they try it on the X-Men."

Clarice was staring at her, wild-eyed. "B-but what will become of you?" she cried. "What will become of you?"

"Ah don't know, girl," Paige answered honestly. "Ah guess it means Ah'm the first to—"

"Enough, *chica!*" Angelo interrupted, grabbing her by the shoulders. "You were right to believe there must be a way out. We can overcome this."

Paige stared at him. What a strange one he was! "Why the change of attitude?" she asked.

"Just because I'm sometimes negative," he said, "doesn't mean I'm not smart enough to hope."

"Hope...?"

They all wheeled around in an instant—all but the catatonic girl. And there, towering over them, looking down at them through a perfectly round hole in the wall of the chamber, was the Phalanx unit called Harvest!

His beard was brown, his eyes were red, and he must have been ten feet tall. His body armor was imposing enough. But what was really frightening were the four heads sticking out of his chest. All of them were screaming, but none of them were making a sound.

"Let me tell you about hope, children," he said, in a hollow, half-mechanical voice. "I was a human being once. My name was...It doesn't matter. I was a man. A husband. A father. My heart was filled to overflowing with hope that the world would be a better place...if I were only brave enough to join the Phalanx and rid that world of mutants.

"But that was when I was a carbonite. Something less than I am now. Now I am called Harvest. And I will not rest until all organic life on the planet Earth has disappeared."

"And we're to sit back while you attack and kill?" Clarice shot back. "No, Harvest...not me!"

As with most mutants, Clarice Ferguson remembered the first time she'd used her mutant ability. She had shattered everything around her—by simply blinking. In that moment, staring at the damage she'd done, she'd vowed never to use her power against another living being.

But now all that changed in the blink of Clarice's eye. For a fraction of an instant, everything that was Harvest was somewhere else! He seemed to shatter like glass, then come back together, screaming in pain.

In that instant, Gregor grabbed Clarice, pulling her away. "Get back, Clarice! He'll hurt you!" he shouted.

"Gregor, no!" she screamed. "Let me go!"

But in the moment that she was held back, the hole in the wall closed again. The last sight the young mutants saw was Harvest reeling back in pain, yet recovering.

They all understood—he would be back.

"Interesting," Angelo said, getting up and stretching. His loose folds of skin tightened around him.

"Holy cow, gang," Gregor said apologetically, releasing Clarice. "I hope I didn't do anything wrong! I was just afraid of what he'd do if he got ahold of Clarice!"

"Don't blame yourself, Gregor," Paige told him comfortingly. "We're all new to this."

Angelo frowned, thinking. "We learned they apparently can't dampen our powers," he said, "or they would have. Which means instead of us being trapped in here with them...they're trapped in here with us."

"I don't care who's trapped with who," Clarice said. "We've got to get out of here!"

"I don't think so, gang," Gregor said, shaking his head. "It'd be safer if we stay put and wait for the X-Men, like Paige said."

"Not me," Clarice said firmly. "I don't agree."

"We need to—" But Angelo was suddenly interrupted by the dark-skinned beauty sitting against the wall. The girl they'd all assumed was totally out of it.

"You need to be quiet," she said.

"*Qué?*" Angelo gasped.

"Golly!" Gregor exclaimed. "Ms. St. Croix, you spoke!"

The girl ignored him. "Our first priority, people," she said, in a tone of absolute certainty, "is to free ourselves from this, the first of many prisons." So saying, she ripped off the shoulder of her dark blue suit.

Gregor shook his head. "While you were in your catatonic stupor—no offense, ma'am—we realized we were trapped pretty darn good. Somehow, the Phalanx is monitoring our every move."

"They were using these techno-organic suits to do it," the girl answered. "But I've just recalibrated the raw material—built something totally new from the old fabric. Now I'm going to use it to help us get out of here. "

Paige's jaw dropped. The girl had transformed the material of the suit instantly into a hard, hammerlike object.

"All I require is a power source," the girl said. "That should be provided by this light."

She smashed the hard object into one of the glowing patches. The patch shattered like glass, and the object in her hand began to glow. Then it became a focused beam of light.

Moving so fast that she seemed like a blur, the girl swung the beam around until it fell on Gregor!

"No!" As the rest of them watched in horror, Gregor's handsome face fell away. His skin melted like wax, revealing the features of a

Phalanx unit, screaming in pain.

"How did you know? How—you—00111100101101101110?"

The four young mutants stood and stared. Gregor began to disintegrate into a puddle of techno-organic matter. Then he exploded all over the chamber!

"Madre de Dios..."

"Whoa..."

"Yucch..."

"He was posing as one of us all along?" Angelo said. "Incredible. How did you know, Monet?"

The dark-skinned beauty knelt and faced the wall of the chamber, already at work on their escape. "There are precious few things I don't know, sir," she replied.

As they watched her, she examined the remains of the Gregor unit. When she was done, she turned around to explain matters to the rest of them.

"Listen closely," she said, "because I only have time to go over this once. The Phalanx were too smart for their own good this time. Harvest placed 'Gregor' here as a plant. But I figured it out from the way Gregor talked. All those old-fashioned expressions he used gave him away.

"Judging by the damage I did to him, I think I've fused open a channel to their core central. They think they still see him here, watching over us. Any questions?"

"Uh...just one," Angelo said. "What the— so you're sayin' you can get us out of here?"

"At the very least," Monet St. Croix replied, "we should be able to escape this particular techno-organic chamber. After that, it will depend entirely on how creative we are when it comes to our survival. Now, if I might have a moment to concentrate...?"

She turned back to the wall, and placed her hands on it.

"But when Harvest entered before," Clarice said, pointing to the far wall, "the door was over there."

"Yes. I know," Monet said. Drawing back her fist, she slammed it through the wall. It shattered, creating a hole big enough for them all to walk through together.

"I'm impressed, *chica*," Angelo said. "But is there a reason you didn't do that earlier?"

"Two spring to mind, Mr. Espinosa," Monet

replied. "If we manage to survive this, I might be willing to discuss them at length. Now, if we could get going...?"

"Certainly," Angelo said. "And, Monet—*gracías*."

"Certainly." She watched as Angelo and Clarice left the chamber, then froze as Paige spoke up.

"Keep an...eye on them...gal..." Paige was kneeling in a corner, holding her stomach.

"Paige?" Monet came slowly toward the kneeling figure. "It's the techno-organic virus, isn't it? The infection is spreading."

"Been fightin' it f'while...but feels like muh gut's on fire," Paige said, breathing with difficulty. "Go on...without...me. Ah'd only...slow y'all up..."

"Totally logical," Monet said. "Your condition certainly puts the rest of us at risk. But until you are dead or assimilated into their covenant, it is a risk I'm willing to take."

Monet held a hand out toward Paige, causing her to rise into the air and float out of the chamber as gently as a feather. Then, Monet followed her outside.

They were on the deck of a ship—a Navy

destroyer. Behind them, the techno-organic bubble seemed smaller than it had been when they were inside it.

Monet stared out at the ocean, glittering black in the moonlight. There were other ships not far away. Apparently, they were in the harbor of some big city or other. Monet could see the lights of tall buildings on the horizon.

"No sign of the Phalanx," Clarice said. "Reason enough to give thanks."

"On the contrary, Ms. Ferguson," Monet corrected her. "We are surrounded on all sides by a hostile life form, capable of using either organic or technological matter to replicate itself. An enemy is out there, in the darkness— waiting for us..."

Before any of them knew what was happening, a Phalanx unit had wrapped its tentacles around Clarice and lifted her high into the air. She screamed in fear and pain, her eyes going from blue to bright white.

It amazed Clarice that these things were once human beings—human beings who had willingly become these connected yet unfeeling monsters.

Clarice should have been able to escape, but she was too frightened. Not only of the creatures who clawed at her, but of her own mutant powers.

She felt a searing flash of pain, and realized that she and her three companions were going to die.

The others were at the base of the Phalanx unit that held her, striking at it furiously. "There is little we can do to free her, short of breaking her in half!" Monet shouted to the others.

"Clarice!" Paige cried out. "You gotta use your powers! You *gotta!*"

"I can't, Paige!" Clarice screamed. "I'm so scared!"

"Do it, girl!" Angelo urged her. "Blink that thing to pieces!"

Clarice cried out in panic, her eyes flared, and a warm glow sliced through her body. She felt her power flow from her, aimed straight at her attacker!

For a moment, there was nothing but silence. And then, the Phalanx unit screamed in agony as its body was segmented by Clarice's phasing pulse.

"You did it, Clarice!" Paige cried triumphantly. Clarice fell, only to be caught in the folds of Angelo's skin.

"It's okay now, sweetie," Paige assured her. "Angelo's got you!"

"Dis-diss-funk-funk-function—systems—massive neural disruption—pain—intense—"

"Really, creature?" Monet St. Croix asked. "Then consider how this feels!"

Monet calmly stepped forward. With one punch, she obliterated the disrupted Phalanx unit. Pieces of it scattered across the rusted deck of the destroyer.

"Wow..." Clarice said softly.

"Niña," Angelo said, "did you kill that man?"

"I haven't a clue, Espinoza," Monet told him. "Who's to say it was even a man? Or truly alive? But did you hear him?" she asked pointedly. "He sounded very different from the other Phalanx we've encountered! Less well formed, somehow..."

"Monet's right," Paige said. "Somethin's weird about these particular Phalanx, on this boat." Then she gasped, looking over her companions' heads as a moonshadow fell across them. "But truth t'tell, gang—oh, my Lord— Ah don't think we're gonna get the chance ta find out what—!"

"You are correct, carbo-mote," Harvest said. "The Phalanx who serve me are ill-formed. You are also correct in saying that you will not live to discover why. For the Harvest time has come—and the crop shall be mutants!

"It is fitting that the last of you will be the first to fall before the culling scythe of the Phalanx!" he roared, towering over Paige.

"Ah know about farmin', y'know," she said calmly, staring up at him unbowed. "And we particular 'crops' ain't ready t'be harvested!"

"Your position is hopeless, female. You and all your kind will fall, mutant—because a new species has risen to replace you!"

Paige stood her ground, continuing to draw him out...continuing to stall... If she could help them survive even a moment longer, it might be enough. She felt certain in her heart that help was on the way—and even if it didn't come, they might somehow find a way out of this mess.

"Hate t'tell you this, Harvest," she said, "but we were born this way—what's your excuse?"

"I was made—transformed! I volunteered

to become that much better than your kind—losing all I had—my family, my humanity, my very life. I gave it all up so I would rise one rung above you on the evolutionary ladder—in order to serve the collective intelligence—the covenant to help eliminate mutants from this world, once and for all!"

"For someone servin' a 'collective,'" Paige said, "you sure say 'me' and 'I' a whole lot!"

"I will not deny that for reasons unknown to me, my access to the Phalanx hive has been severed. But this isolation will not prevent me from achieving my goal—and nothing and no one will stop me!"

He rose up to his full, awesome height and raised a huge arm over Paige's head.

"Oh, my Lord," Paige whispered, realizing that the moment of truth was at hand. Harvest was clearly through talking. There was no way she could hold off her fate much longer. "X-Men—if you're out there, please—please *hurry!*"

On the outside of the ship's hull lay the anchor chain, sloping down into the water. And at that very moment, Banshee and

Everett were climbing up it.

"Quietly, Everett, m'lad," Banshee instructed. "We don't know how many o' the Phalanx creatures are here or where they are—but I do hear one o' them above."

"That's quite a pair of ears you got, Banshee," Everett said admiringly.

Banshee smiled down at him as they climbed. "With me powers bein' what they are, son, it's either hear very well or be deaf, aye?" he asked.

They got to the top of the chain, and entered the ship through the hole in the hold.

"We're in!" Banshee whispered. "Once we targeted this area, finding where the beasties had taken the young mutants wasn't difficult. There've been mysterious disappearances of people reported along these docks. And with what we've learned from the other X-Men units—that the Phalanx seem t'like heights an' large metallic objects—this old ship seemed the only place they could be.

"Now the task is t'find the others like yourself who've been captured by these creatures, and pray that Emma Frost and Jubilee had as little trouble finding their way aboard as we did."

♦   ♦   ♦

"You get a brain-tap on anythin' yet, Frosty?" Jubilee and Emma Frost were down in the area of the engine room. It was pitch dark.

"If you are asking whether I have telepathically located the kidnapped mutants—the answer is yes. They are together—but very upset and very frightened. I am also picking up Phalanx signals, but not like those we've encountered before."

"Well," Jubilee said, stretching out her hands, "I'll send some sparkles up to shed some light on the sitch—and would you mind speaking plain English, please?"

Paff! The shower of sparkles lit up the interior of the ship's hold, and Jubilee and Emma Frost found themselves staring at dozens of techno-organic rats!

"I'm not sure what I find more horrific, Jubilee," the White Queen said, her hand in front of her mouth, "your use of language—or that the Phalanx are desperate enough to include rats in their collective!"

"Eeyaagh!" Jubilee screeched. "Major grossout! But I can paff these rats inta Mickeypizza"—*shapaff!*—"an' I won't feel guilty about it!"

Emma Frost smiled at her—the first time Jubilee had ever seen her smile. "So is that why you've held back on using your mutant abilities?" she asked. "For fear of hurting someone?"

"Uhm...I practically blew up a whole house in Hong Kong once, y'know," Jubilee admitted.

"And you worry about what would happen

if you ever unleashed your powers?" Emma asked her. "It's perfectly understandable for you to be a little afraid, Jubilee—your potential is incredible."

Emma's expression grew suddenly thoughtful, even sad. "By the same token," she said, "perhaps it's time that people like me see to it that youngsters like you are better taught and trained than the previous group of young mutants—we owe them that much, at least. That is, of course, if we can keep your generation alive!"

"I know it sounds crazy," Angelo said as the four young mutants cowered against the bulkhead of the ship. "But does anyone else hear fireworks?"

Harvest reared up in front of them—bigger and bigger, closer and closer.

"It is the sound of futility you hear, carbonite! The X-Men have arrived to try and rescue you—but they shall not succeed!"

Grrrrr...

"What was that sound—Sabretooth!"

Harvest had guessed right, but not before the claws came flashing, severing Harvest's blaster from the arm which held it!

"Paige," Angelo said, "is *this* one o' the X-Men you said was gonna be savin' us?"

"Well, he's definitely not Wolverine," Paige replied. "Sabretooth, he said? Errrr...he's no X-Man Ah ever saw, gang."

"You got that right, frail," Sabretooth roared as he struck again, ripping a techno-organic arm from its socket. "An' you better be grateful for that!"

"Ultimately, your savagery is pointless, Sabretooth," Harvest said with a horrible, hollow laugh. "For every limb you rend, two will take its place!"

"Guess it just means I'll haveta start rippin' 'em off four at a time, eh?" Sabretooth returned.

"Well dealt, butcher, but I can draw techno-organic matter back from those whom I have assimilated...and then we shall see who exhausts himself first."

Clarice watched in terror as Harvest grew two new tentacles. "Oh, no...he's getting even bigger—how can we stop him?" she cried.

But just then, a scream that none of them had ever heard split the night—and Harvest exploded into pieces!

"This X-Man I know, gang," Paige told her friends excitedly, "and Banshee is definitely here to rescue us!"

"That I am, lass," Banshee said, appearing from a doorway with a young black man behind him. "An' I brought along some help as well. Meet Everett Thomas. He's like all o' ye."

"But better," Everett corrected him.

"I'm surprised to find you here, Creed," Banshee said.

"Got a problem with it, Irish?"

"Not at all, boyo."

"Good," Sabretooth said, surveying the techno-organic wreckage around him with satisfaction. "If it weren't for me, these punks would be history!"

"In light o' the fact they're all livin' and breathin'," Banshee said, "I'd say that not only do I agree with ye, but we're in yuir debt as well. I'm not happy about it, to be sure, but the kids are safe. Tell me, Creed—how'd ye find us?"

"I got my ways, Irish. Had 'em for a long time 'fore I became Xavier's 'patient,' too."

Paige stepped forward. "Mr. Cassidy, sir," she said, "Ah'm Paige Guthrie—Sam's sister. All of us were kidnapped by the Phalanx, and—"

"I think they've pretty much figured that part out," Angelo interrupted her.

"I know who ye are, lass," Banshee said, a look of concern coming over his face. "But what's happened to you?"

"Paige was infected by that Harvest guy,"

Angelo explained. "The transmode virus has been spreading through her ever since!"

Suddenly, Sabretooth stepped forward, and, putting his face next to Paige's, began sniffing!

"Why is he smelling me?" Paige asked nervously.

"Ya got two scents, girlie," Sabretooth answered, raising a hand and extending his claws. "An' I got a pretty good idea why!"

Shakkashgth!

Down came the claw, slicing right through Paige's face, through her chest and abdomen.

"Creed!" Banshee gasped in horror. "What're ye doing, man? If ye've hurt the girl, I'll—"

"You'll what, Cassidy?" Sabretooth roared, stepping back from Paige, who stood there, stock still. "All I did t'the frail is save her life!"

They watched in stunned silence as Paige Guthrie tore out of her own skin! She feverishly removed the layer of skin infected by the techno-organic mesh—like corn being shucked of its husk—until the young girl's mutant powers stood revealed.

Paige's skin—if you could call it that—was

flesh no longer. It gleamed like metal in the moonlight.

"So what're y'all lookin' at?" Paige demanded, glaring at them all, her eyes glowing red in the night. "It's kinda weird, I know, but it's what I do—okay? Don't stare *too* hard. I'll be back to normal in a few hours!"

"Creed, that was a big risk ye took!" Banshee scolded him.

"Risk?" Sabretooth repeated. "For her, maybe, Irish. Not me. No skin off my nose!"

Everett spoke up. "Mr. Cassidy," he said nervously, "I think we're forgetting one thing here. If your sonic scream destroyed Harvest— shouldn't it have withered this girl's techno-organic mesh as well?"

"Of course it should have, child! That is— assuming Banshee's wail had accomplished its intended task—which it most certainly *did not!*"

"Fall back!" Banshee ordered, as Harvest rose again from the rubble of his body parts. "Scatter! Don't give him any stationary targets!"

"Your attempts at survival are useless, mutant! I am whole again, having taken back all techno-matter in the vicinity. And while I may remain isolated from the collective will of the Phalanx, my fundamental reason for existence has not changed! If mutants cannot be assimilated—they must be eliminated!"

As Harvest spoke, he discharged from his body the four figures that had seemed to be a part of it. They fell to the deck of the ship.

"Move away from there!" Clarice shouted to them. But the figures remained still and lifeless.

"Oh, no, no, no..." Clarice moaned. "Those people—they're all dead! He—he killed them all—so he could be stronger...and kill us. What kind of a person would do something like this?"

"It is not a person we're fighting, Clarice," Monet said.

"It's not indeed!" Banshee agreed, taking to the air and hovering over the scene. "Now—*move!*"

Down below decks, Jubilee and Emma Frost were still fighting their way through an army of techno-rodents.

"Continue your attack, Jubilee!" the White

Queen urged. "You have to buy us time! I'm going to contact Banshee telepathically!"

"Do your stuff, Frosty," Jubilee told her, sending fireworks popping out at the monstrous rats. "An' I'll do mine!"

Emma Frost began her probe, and soon was transmitting a psi-message to Banshee. At his request, she was able to determine that Harvest was completely Phalanx—body and soul. Her psi-probe showed no sign of human thought patterns.

But he's still able to counter our mutant powers, Banshee reported. *So what's our plan, Ms. Frost?*

I should think that would be obvious, she told him telepathically. *First thing we do is get the children off this ship.*

My thoughts exactly, Emma. I'll distract Harvest. You get the kids to safety.

Right.

Their psi-communication complete, Banshee turned his attention back to the matter at hand. "Creed!" he shouted. "We need a frontal assault, boyo! Go to town!"

"Irish," Sabretooth replied, already in mid-leap, "y'know, if this keeps up, I might just get t'the point where I won't hate yer guts any-more!"

"Oh, joy," Banshee replied dryly, checking out the rolling ball of fur and flying techno-parts that was Sabretooth and Harvest. Banshee dove in, screaming.

Clarice looked on in sheer horror. "They—they'll both be hurt!" she gasped.

"They know exactly what they're doing, my dear." Clarice turned to find a beautiful blond woman and a teenage girl with short, dark hair facing her. It was the blond woman who had spoken. "I'm Emma Frost. And this is Jubilee. Now I must ask you all to come with us at once."

"Yeah?" Jubilee spoke up. "Well, I'm not leaving Banshee behind, Frosty!"

At that moment, Harvest rose from the tangle, with Sabretooth in one huge tentacle and Banshee in the other! "You will fall, mutants! Your blood shall be wiped clean so you shall never soil the people of this planet again! First you—then your precious next generation!"

With a ferocious squeeze, Harvest choked Sabretooth until he was limp. Then he threw

Creed to the deck, where he collapsed in a heap. Monet ran to him and knelt down to see if he was still alive. Meanwhile, up above, Banshee took on Harvest so the others could make their escape.

Clarice turned to Emma Frost and wiped away a tear. "Ma'am," she said, "Harvest— can't be stopped, can it? I mean, even if we do get away today, it'll keep coming after us, won't it?"

"It will," Emma acknowledged. "We are simply delaying the inevitable."

Clarice swallowed hard. "Then...it has to be stopped, right?" she asked. She was choking back soft sobs now, and the tears were streaming down her cheeks. "I mean, right now...doesn't it? I mean—just because we're mutants, it wants to kill us. And after it's done that, it'll just find other mutants to kill. And then, when all mutants are dead—regular humans will be next, right?"

"Well, yes," Everett spoke up. "But do you have to make it sound so depressing?"

"Sabretooth is still alive, people," Monet informed them. "But he's unconscious."

"Let's be rational here, Clarice," Paige said,

taking the crying girl by the shoulders. "We can't stop Harvest right now—we don't have the firepower!"

Clarice stared back at her, her eyes clear with purpose, even though they were still tear-stained.

"No, Paige," she said, "that's where I think you're wrong. Because I think—maybe—I *do* have the strength and the power. I just never had the guts. But until now, I'd never seen the kind of blind hatred Harvest represents! I'd never seen people with the courage to sacrifice everything so that others could live!"

And with that, she broke from Paige's grip and ran toward Harvest.

"Clarice—*stop!*" Paige screamed. "You can't beat him!"

Clarice turned to look back at them all once more. "You know I can, Paige," she said, the tears still flowing, but her face sure and determined. "Goodbye, my friends. I hope what I'm going to do makes a difference... somewhere down the road."

Blink!

Suddenly, the deck they were standing on gave way beneath them, and they were falling through the air. "Look out!" Emma Frost cried. "She's teleported a slice of the deck and ship's hull out from under us!"

"She was savin' our lives," Angelo said as they fell, "knowin' there would be nothin' any of us could do to stop her if we were all in the water!"

Back on the deck, Clarice ran toward Harvest. Banshee was struggling with the huge techno-monster, barely holding his own.

"Girl, are ye daft?" he cried when he saw Clarice approaching. "Get away from here!"

"I'm sorry, Mr. Banshee, sir," Clarice replied, reaching out a hand and touching Harvest's head. "But I can stop this monster— here and now and forever."

Blink!

"Can you now, mutant filth? Eh? What is— happening—to me? Why am I—incapable of analyzing—predictable patterns—to these spatial-shearing—mutagenic energies?"

"Clarice!" Banshee cried. Freed of Harvest's grip, he took to the air. "Come here—quickly, now! Before ye're trapped by yer own powers!"

But Clarice wasn't listening. Closer and closer she came to the quivering form of

Harvest, as the shattered pieces of him came back together.

"Systems breakdown—imminent—filthy—misbegotten—mutant—scum—"

"Reach for my hand!" Banshee yelled, grabbing her wrist. "I won't let ye go, child! I won't!"

"I—I can't—feel—anything—" Clarice said, her body slowly coming apart like the Phalanx unit's.

Blink!

The great ship shattered into a thousand pieces.

"Oh, God—" Banshee cried, as the hand he was gripping so tightly splintered too. "Hang on—please...Lord, don't do this t'her! I can't—find—yuir—fingers—*Nnooooooo!*"

Sean Cassidy fell, with a wrenching sonic scream. It wasn't the wail of his mutant powers that echoed over the roar of sucking air and sliced metal—but the sounds of a man whose heart had just been broken.

Emma Frost shook her head sadly as she and the others watched Clarice disappear. They were floating in a lifeboat that had fallen into the water with them.

"Their poor, tortured souls!" Emma said. "I felt the psychic cries from both of them. Clarice...is gone. We've got to reach Sean Cassidy quickly—before he drowns! We've lost Clarice—and losing one ally today is payment enough!"

Everett flew over and plucked Banshee from the water. "I got you, Mr. Cassidy!" he shouted as they flew back to the lifeboat. "Harvest is gone—ripped out of existence! We did it!"

Then he corrected himself. "*She* did it," he said somberly.

Soon, they were back in the lifeboat and rowing to shore. While Emma Frost tended to Banshee, the five young mutants turned to each other for warmth and comfort. They talked in whispers, unable to believe what had happened.

The world was no longer a simple place for these five, but they knew now that they each had a responsibility to make it a safe one. The lesson had cost them the life of a girl who might have been their friend...and their inno-cence.

Would that price be too steep for tomorrow's mutants? Thanks to one of them, they would have the rest of their lives to find out.

Banshee and Emma Frost looked over at the children they had helped to save. One battle was done. Another, even bigger battle, was about to begin.

Though one of their own had died, there was hope now. Hope that the Phalanx could be beaten.

And when that day came—*if* it came—there would be the children to teach, raise, and protect.

If Emma and Banshee did their jobs right, the world would always have X-Men to shield and preserve its people—mutant and human alike.

⊗ ⊗ **Interlude** ⊗ ⊗

The Phalanx attack on Muir Island came suddenly, without warning. Professor Charles Xavier was barely able to get to the Communications Room. Securing the door behind him, he immediately called for help.

The Muir Island Cerebro unit quickly located Wolverine in Canada. Xavier signaled him to come to Muir Island right away and help find the missing X-Men.

Cable was next. Xavier knew that the head of X-Force had the perfect qualifications to meet the Phalanx threat head-on.

But there were others to alert. Without them, even the combined powers of Cable and Wolverine wouldn't be enough to save the missing X-Men.

Xavier used Cerebro to locate Cyclops and Jean Grey. *Scott...Jean...* he signaled the new-lywed couple.

I hear you, Professor, Jean's voice sounded inside his head.

I'm at Muir—we're under attack. The X-Men are missing! The Phalanx has—

But before he could finish, the door was smashed in and two Phalanx units burst into the room. One of them had Moira McTaggart in its tentacles!

The professor cut off the communication, hoping Jean had heard enough to understand his message. Instantly, he turned all his attention to freeing Moira.

With a powerful psi-blast, he forced the Phalanx unit to drop her. As she hit the ground, Xavier fought off the two units with his telepathic powers.

Moira ran to his arms. Xavier guided his hoverchair out of the room and down into the tunnels beneath the center.

Xavier was sure that the four mutants he'd contacted would make up the best team for tracking down the missing X-Men.

But there was more to be done than simply finding Storm and her kidnapped team. Professor X knew that the Phalanx presented a danger bigger than any other.

He knew from the psi-signals he'd picked up that the invaders were setting up bases across the Earth. It was going to take all his mutants to fight against this global threat.

X-Force, X-Factor, and Excalibur would all be needed to destroy the Phalanx bases.

"Charles, they're gainin' on us!" Moira cried as the hoverchair sped toward the underground boat dock, where a speedboat lay waiting for them. Xavier revved the motor and they raced away, narrowly escaping the grasping tentacles of the Phalanx!

"Where will we go, Charles?" she asked him as the black cliffs of Muir Island disappeared from sight.

"To my secret sanctuary in the abandoned monastery of Mont Saint Francis, off the northern coast of France," he told her. "When we get there, I'll alert the others. Those monsters may have taken over Muir Island, Moira—but we're not through fighting yet!"

⊗ ⊗ ⊗ **10** ⊗ ⊗ ⊗

"It's too quiet down there, Scott." Jean Grey and Scott Summers were at the controls of a supersonic jet aircraft, high over Muir Island. "Total communications silence, psionic or otherwise! But Professor Xavier is supposed to be here. His emergency message said so. What could have—"

"Do you see that, Jean?" Scott said, pointing. "There seems to be something over the whole lab complex...something like...like..."

But words failed him. For what Scott

Summers saw before him was like nothing he had ever seen before. They were the Phalanx— and they had made Muir Island one of their first conquests on Earth.

"Full extension, Egon. Intercept the mutants while Nkotha and I attack from the side!"

"They are mine, Larissa!"

"No, Egon—they are ours!"

Jean Grey winced, and turned to her husband. On their honeymoon, they had been psionically pulled two thousand years into the future. There, they had spent years helping to save the world from Apocalypse. Now they had returned—to find only a week had gone by. But in the week they'd been gone, a lot had certainly happened!

"I'm picking up a load of fierce psi-babble, Scott," she said. "As if three maniacs were screaming at the same time! Whatever they are, they're herding us toward that big thing at ten o'clock high! What in the world is that, anyway?"

"Hang on, Jean," Scott said, pushing down on the throttle. "I'm going down hard!"

The swift downward plunge of the aircraft

fooled the Phalanx unit long enough for them to avoid it and make a hard landing. The plane skidded to a stop right in front of the research center's main entrance.

"Get out, Jean! Quickly!"

"Scott—look out!"

Just as they got clear, a huge techno-organic fist crashed down on their airplane, smashing it to bits! The creature reared up above them, balancing on its tentacles. It raised its arms together over its head, ready to strike again.

"If you can 'hear' them, can they 'hear' you?" Scott asked his wife.

"Probably," Jean answered. "That's why I'm blocking them—but it's like peeking through a keyhole while trying to keep the door closed!"

"Maybe a dose of optic blast will distract them long enough—" He raised the ruby quartz visor that covered his eyes. As long as he wore it, the visor contained the power of Cyclops's awesome optic blasts. Now he sent one directly at the Phalanx unit!

The unit absorbed the blow, then quickly recovered.

"No good," Jean said. "If you tell me what you're doing, and even a little bit of what I'm thinking leaks through my psi-block, these—these beings can counter our next move! Scott, the island seems *infested*—what happened to the Professor and Moira?"

Meanwhile, an airplane appeared on the horizon. It was an old World War II army plane. With smoke trailing from its rusting engines, it flew slowly toward the fight. Scott and Jean looked at each other hopefully. Could it be...?

The pilot of the plane turned toward his lone passenger. "Something's scanning us with high-power stuff across the whole spectrum," he told Wolverine. "But we probably aren't registering! We're so low-tech that the high-end stuff looks right through us. But whatever it is, it's burning out all my instruments. Whatever's down there is hairy to the max, Logan!"

"But down there is where I gotta be, Harry!" Wolverine told the pilot as he tightened the straps of his parachute. "You can refuel in Scotland and scoot on home...oh, and thanks for the lift!" And with that, he was gone, plummeting earthward.

The sound of his parachute opening drew the attention of the Phalanx unit called Larissa. *"What?"* she gasped.

"Heads up, circuit-face!" Wolverine yelled, his bone claws extended for business. "The ol' Canucklehead is back in town, and somebody's gonna pay!"

"Egon and Nkotha, deal with the other mutants. I'll deal with this new one!"

She turned on Wolverine, but he was ready for her. Claws slashed across the techno-organic neck, severing the head. "You stick yer mug where it don't belong, it's gonna get ripped!" he shouted.

But from the neck grew several long tentacles, each with a hideous head on its end! They wrapped themselves around Wolverine, squeezing so tightly he could hardly breathe.

"If that is the best you can do, mutant, then this entity of Phalanx will make short work of you!"

Wolverine grimaced in pain. "Charles told me this was gonna be a tough one," he grunted. "I said, 'It ain't Magneto, is it?' He said, 'No.' I said, 'So what are ya worried about?' Now I know."

"You are a stain on the surface of this planet, mutant—a purely organic defect that Phalanx will soon correct."

"You should talk about bein' defective, lady," Wolverine shot back, freeing himself quickly with his bone claws. "You're all over the place!"

Almost immediately, the pieces of Larissa began to reform themselves. Wolverine braced for another vicious attack.

Cyclops and Jean heard the commotion. Finishing off their opponents, they turned to see what the noise was all about.

"Jean—do you see—it's Wolverine!" Cyclops shouted. "Look out, Logan—I'm aiming high!" And with that, he shot an optic blast at the creature.

"Scott!" Jean yelled, trying to warn him. "You shouldn't have said—" But she stopped short, as Cyclops's blast hammered home, hitting the Larissa unit dead center.

"He was fakin 'em out, Jean," Wolverine explained as he fell out of the creature's grasp and plummeted toward the ground. "That blast came in low!"

Just in the nick of time, Jean sent a psychic

net his way, breaking Wolverine's fall. "You've got to watch it, Logan," she said as he landed softly on a blob of pink energy. "You don't have your adamantium skeleton any longer. That fall could've—"

"Aw, Red," Wolverine stopped her. "I had a feelin' you'd be ready with a psi-cushion!"

He had loved her with all his heart. And that heart had nearly been broken when she'd decided to marry Scott. But Scott Summers was one of Wolverine's best friends. As badly as he felt, Logan had to admit that Jean had chosen well.

"So what's goin' on down here?" he asked them. "I got a mind-blast from Charley Xavier to meet up with him on Muir Island—he seemed almost scared!"

"You know as much as we do," Jean told him "It's...it's good to see you again, Logan. You were missed."

"Sorry," Cyclops interrupted. "No time for reunions right now, folks. These Phalanx things have worked themselves into the very structure of the main lab building. We want to put as much distance as possible between us and them."

"You call the shots, Scott," Logan said, running behind him with Jean bringing up the rear. "It's been a long time since I was a team player."

Meanwhile, inside the main lab building, the Phalanx units that had taken over Muir Island were slowly recovering.

"Reorganize and regroup," said Larissa, their leader. "This threat must be ended. We must heal ourselves, and contact the main consciousness to alert them of the danger here!"

"We have priorities, Larissa," the unit known as Nkotha argued. "We have our mission. We must not divert our main energies from our primary objective: the infiltration and absorption of all Muir Island genetic hardware and data banks!"

"Nkotha and I can maintain hardware and data bank links while holding off the mutants," the Egon unit suggested. "The main consciousness is too far away to—"

"Formulate your attack plans," Larissa said, ignoring Egon's and Nkotha's objections. "I will extend to the main consciousness and merge/share/transfer—"

Stretching herself into an elongated form and acting as an antenna, the Larissa unit closed her eyes and calmed herself. "Submerge into ether matrix. Go digital. Set protocols. Send data. Transfer Phalanx core central—completed! Central designate Lang—I am here to download unit regarding the Muir Island situation—"

Inside the web that was core central, the unit that had been Dr. Stephen Lang was in the middle of interrelating with the mutant designated Psylocke. He was irritated by the interruption of his important work.

"Parameters understood, Larissa. Now is not the time." Ignoring her and turning to the Hodge unit, he said, "Mutagenic physiology still resistant to assimilation process."

"Her psionic powers are weakened, but still considerably dangerous!" the Hodge unit replied.

"More psi-dampers, Hodge—quickly!"

"It is well known that mutants cannot be absorbed, designate Lang," Larissa broke in.

"I know that, Larissa. All the more reason we must secure their number. Now, what are you doing here, Larissa?"

"I came to merge/share. I possess data—"

"No!" Lang quickly retreated from the interface with Larissa. During the merge/share, she had had access to his most private thoughts! What had she seen while he was distracted with Psylocke and had his blocks down? Did she know? Did she suspect?

He had to get rid of her! "Unit override command: return to Muir now!"

There. She was gone. Hodge had returned with the psi-dampers. Everything was as it had been before.

The only question in Lang's mind was— had he gotten rid of Larissa in time?

⊗ ⊗ ⊗ **11** ⊗ ⊗ ⊗

Wolverine sat on a redwood picnic table, facing Jean Grey, as Scott Summers stood a little way off, scouting their position.

The three of them had managed to escape to the remote weather station at the far end of Muir Island. From here, they could see across the rugged cliffs of the shoreline to the Mutant Research Center.

"Sorry about missin' the weddin', Jean," Wolverine said. "I was—"

"Logan," she replied tenderly, "your heart

was there, and that's what's important. It all seems so long ago."

"'S funny you should say that, darlin'. It's like the light in yer eyes is a lot older. Like they been lookin' at a lot more life than it's possible to see in the last few months..."

Jean sighed. "It's harder to hide secrets from you than it is from a psi-talent, Logan," she said. "We were on our honeymoon, when suddenly we were psionically transported two thousand years into the future! We'd been brought there to help defeat Apocalypse, who was the emperor of the entire planet!"

"Give me a break," Wolverine groaned.

"Don't worry, we took care of it," Jean assured him. "Things looked pretty bleak for a while there, but we found Scott's son Nathan. It took ten years to raise him so he'd be old enough to defeat Apocalypse!"

"Whoa, slow down!" Wolverine said, his head spinning. "Lay this on me again—slower this time."

She was about to tell him the whole story— but just then, there was a rumbling beneath the ground. Suddenly, two Phalanx units erupted into the air before them.

"You are only prolonging the inevitable, mutants! We will gather the biological information we desire," one of them said.

"The trunk line!" Scott gasped, staring at the electrical transformer that led to the buried line. "Good Lord! They traveled through the underground cable that connects this weather station to the main lab! Wha—?"

Fwakk! Thoom!

Two blasts split the air around them, obliterating the Phalanx units.

"Force beams?" Scott said, stunned. "Some sort of plasma weapon? Who—?"

And then, turning, he saw who it was. His jaw dropped in astonishment.

The newcomer carried two humongous weapons, and his left eye glowed with orange fire.

"I thought I heard you mention my name as I was bodysliding in," the man said. "Or were you talking about another Cable?"

"You!" Wolverine exclaimed.

"Nate!" Jean cried. It was a sight she had seen many times before—Cable to the rescue. But after all she'd been through recently, she would never see this man quite the same way again. Not ever.

He looked like the Cable she knew—with no sign of the techno-organic transmode virus he'd been so badly infected with by Apocalypse. He had learned to overcome it, and had obviously regained his former strength—but Jean knew he would never be quite whole.

She knew what Cable must never know—that he was the boy they'd raised two thousand years in the future! That she and Scott were "Redd" and "Slym," the parents who had left Nathan alone in the future when they were tugged back into the present day!

"We've got the advantage now!" Cable yelled, reminding them that there was work to be done. "Hit 'em with everything you've got!"

As they fought off the Phalanx units, Jean contacted Scott telepathically.

Scott...Nathan's psi-print is stronger—more in sync with my own than ever before!

Jean—somehow I feel it, too, but we can't talk now—just concentrate on blasting the Phalanx!

"There is yet another mutant enemy! It is best we retreat back to the research center."

The two units were gone as quickly as they had arrived. "That certainly sent them packing," Cable remarked.

"Not another step, bub," Wolverine said belligerently, "until we got proof you are who you appear to be."

Given the Phalanx's ability to morph into human form, it was the only safe move. At any rate, it didn't bother Cable. "Listen, Logan," he said, "I got the same message from Xavier you did. I know what's going on!"

"Logan!" Jean said, coming up to him. "This is Cable! Trust me. I know."

"Xavier didn't have time to explain things very well," Cable told his comrades. "He only said that a race of techno-organic beings from who-knows-where have kidnapped most of the X-Men—and that he'd nominated us to find them, while he an' the others took on the Phalanx on other fronts."

"The X-Men were the first target, as you say," Jean told him. "Based on the vague images I picked up from Larissa and the other Phalanx units here, they seem to be—as they claim—a collective intelligence, one unit linked to the other. They mean to replace all life on this planet with their own. It was a strong feeling I picked up—so strong, it was like it was built into their genes!"

"That would explain why they're here, then," Cyclops said. "Muir is the foremost biological research facility on Earth. Where better to find out about Earth's life forms? They're obviously trying to access the computer core, which the Professor must have shut down before he and the others evacuated—and we need that core so Cerebro can locate the missing X-Men."

"That's assumin' they're still alive, Cyke," Wolverine pointed out.

"Which we won't know for sure," Cable interjected, "until we stick our heads in the lion's mouth. Again."

He frowned, deep in thought. "They're a collective intelligence, right? Okay—with Jean's telepathy to confuse them, and me backing her up, we'll get inside their group mind and really mess 'em up. That should allow Cyke and Logan about five minutes to get in and out of the facility with the info we need!"

"Cable," Jean objected, "with your techno-

organic infection, you'll be especially suscepti-
ble to the Phalanx. You'll have to use extreme
caution."

Cable's jaw dropped. "My—! How did you
know?"

"C'mon, bub, be a sport!" Wolverine said,
giving him a friendly punch on the arm. "Let's
just do it, eh?"

"Right," Cable said, nodding. "Let's just do
it."

He grabbed Jean's hand and they stepped
forward, moving toward the main lab building.

"You be careful out there...the both of
you!" Scott called after his wife and son.

"Don't worry, Cyclops," Cable shouted
back, "charging headlong is sort of my spe-
cialty!"

Jean Grey looked at the man whose hand
she was holding. In another lifetime, in another era, she had raised the boy who had become
this man—nursed him until he overcame the
transmode virus that nearly killed him—
brought him up and trained him until he was
strong enough to destroy Apocalypse and free
the Earth...

But Cable did not recognize her as the woman he had called Redd. Jean had been in a borrowed body then. What would happen to Cable if he found out?

What am I doing? Jean asked herself. When they entered the Phalanx collective consciousness together, Nate would have access to all her most secret memories!

There were things that a son should never know about his parents. Especially if it meant that the future would then change, and he might never even exist!

But was it even possible to avoid those memories? Jean didn't know. She could only hope so—and proceed.

"Are you ready?" she asked him when they came within psi-range.

"Yes," he replied. And then a memory flooded into his consciousness...of himself and Redd, holding hands.

"Try it, Nathan..." Redd was urging him.

"But it's painful..." the boy he had been replied. "I can't, Redd!"

He must have said the last words out loud, for Jean said, "Shhh. Concentrate! Create that clear white spot in the center of your consciousness and let yourself flow through it—let yourself flow!"

And he did. *This is amazing!* he cried, as he felt his essence flying alongside hers through some psychic web of inner space. *I feel like I can do anything!*

Yes, Nate, Jean told him with a smile. *Anything you can imagine!*

Meanwhile, within the main lab building, Larissa had come out of her trance.

"Larissa!" the Nkotha unit called out to her from the main computer banks, where he was busily engaged in downloading information. "Larissa, you have returned from your merge/share with the main! Merge, so I can experience your ecstatic joining with central shared consciousness at the citadel!"

"There was no merge/share!" Larissa told him. "Something is awry! Something is hidden! Share my memory of it!"

"I see/hear/smell/feel it! Lang is holding back! He is not sharing! Lang is a partial absorbee...he remained mostly human to be our interface with the non-cyber world. He is not truly techno-organic. We must alert the main collective and initiate—"

"No time! The mutant female is a powerful psi, and the newest arrival is dangerous also! We must carry out our mission before they—"

Larissa stopped in mid-sentence, sensing something wrong. A new presence was invading the space...

"—They come!"

*She/he/they have entered our consciousness!
Regroup/merge/internalize!*

They were inside now—inside the
Phalanx's collective consciousness.

*My every thought is a flashing beam of sizzling
power!* Cable cried out. *This is incredible, Jean! I
feel such an ecstatic wholeness in this state of
being. It's as if I were riding an avalanche of lim-
itless power!*

*Don't let yourself get carried away within the
astral plane, Cable,* Jean warned him. *It's tempt-*

ing, I know. But you have to concentrate!

The Phalanx units screamed in panic and agony. *We are not prepared for an attack from within! She/he/they are unmaking us!*

I can blast them with pure pain! Cable thought.

Keep your bearings, Cable, Jean told him. *Look for weak spots!*

Look for weak spots, Nkotha! We cannot be defeated! We are the final solution!

We don't have any weak spots, Larissa! Cable shouted telepathically.

Again Jean warned him. *Power alone won't win here, Cable. Hold back a reserve! Use strategy!* But now, it wasn't Jean talking to him—it was Redd!

Redd? No! How can it be?

Nate! You do as I say! she ordered. But the change in Cable had not gone unnoticed.

Here is the weak spot! Larissa told her companions. *There is a key memory sequence from the carbonite unit's childhood. It is causing a glitch in their psi-linkage! Nkotha—you concentrate on the she/entity, while I press the attack on the techno-organic infectee and commence the absorption process!*

Arrggh! Cable screamed. *Jean—Redd—help!*

Concentrate, Nate! Focus! You're letting them through!

How did you come to have those memories from my childhood? he demanded. *How—unless—?*

You're letting them through! Find your center, Nate! Get it back together!

But Cable would not—could not obey. *Tell me!* he shouted. *How did you know?*

Jean fought off both Nkotha and Larissa while she attempted to explain things to Cable. *When we entered the Phalanx collective consciousness, we went through a mind-share. I was connected for an instant to all your memories. And now they are imprinted on my cortex!*

It was a lie, of course. But if it would allow Cable to focus, to resume the fight, Jean knew it couldn't be wrong.

Merge with me, Nkotha, Larissa ordered, and her subordinate obeyed, fusing his mass and power with hers. *They are intrinsically non-collective! They quibble, they vacillate, and they argue. They are no match for a unified consciousness!*

Jean! Cable gasped as he felt himself being

thrown head-over-heels, *they're...too...strong!*

Not if we counter with a mind-bond! Jean told him. *We have to focus on a shared memory—a moment of strength! Don't worry, Nathan...*

And as he listened, Jean's voice became Redd's...they were walking over a bridge...Apocalypse's guards were waiting for them. Would they discover that Nate, Redd, and Slym weren't humans after all—but mutants?

"Do not fear, Nathan Dayspring," Redd was telling him. "Fear will weaken the psi-blocks, dim our disguise."

"Papers!" the guard ordered. "Where are your papers?"

"They're just ordinary soldiers, Nate," Redd assured him.

But then, Nate let go of Redd's hand for an instant, and the guard saw him as he really was. "What's wrong with the lad's arm?" he demanded, seeing through the telepathic disguise and noticing the techno-organic web growing there.

"There's nothing wrong with him," Redd insisted, taking Nate's hand again. Instantly, the skin was back, covering the truth.

"Oh, Redd, I slipped," Nate moaned. "I—"

"Don't worry, Nathan," Redd told him, shielding him with her body. "I'll get us through this..."

The words echoed in Cable's head as he heard Jean Grey shout, *I'll get us through this! Remember the moment, Nathan! Use the power of it! Let it well up inside like an unstoppable force—and unleash it!*

Eeeeeyaaaaah! They have a mind-bond! It is strong enough to backlash along our mind-net—to Egon!

The Egon unit was accessing the main Cerebro unit when Wolverine and Cyclops burst in. They saw the computer console—just as Egon saw them!

"You dare to penetrate the inner core of a Phalanx-co-opted structure? Genetic anomaly vermin!"

"What's he doing here?" Cyclops wondered. "Jean and Cable are supposed to have them all wrapped up!"

"He's winding up for a swing, Cyke!" Wolverine warned. "Gotta move!"

And move they did—just in the nick of

time. "You get ready to optic-blast his ugly mug, Cyclops," Wolverine said, "while the ol' Canucklehead keeps him occupied!" Turning to the Egon unit, he shouted, "Come on, spaghetti-face! Let's go to claw city!"

He leaped at the thing, but met no resistance—until he found himself gripped in a gigantic tentacle! "I knew this was too easy," he grunted as it squeezed him. "Zap him, Scott!"

"I can't, Logan!" came the reply. "He's using you as a shield!"

"Better think o' somethin' fast, Cyke," Wolverine grunted, grimacing. "This is startin' to hurt!"

But just then, the mind-bond between Jean and Cable kicked in. The sudden shift startled the Egon unit. It dropped Wolverine from its grasp.

"Go for it, Scott!" Wolverine yelled. "While he's reelin'!"

"Will do!" Cyclops replied, running for Cerebro. "I'm going for the access switch!"

"*Eeeeyaaaa!* Larissa/Nkotha—the genetic anomalies are raiding the Cerebro unit!"

✦ ✦ ✦

But Larissa/Nkotha was in no shape to respond. The combined unit had problems of its own.

Arr! They've fooled us—drawn us out with the queen and a knight while their bishop and rook advanced! Let's see how you play after we knock all the pieces off the board!

Jean! What are they—?

Get behind me, Nate! she ordered. *They're coming after you!*

The psionic blast hit Cable full force, throwing him into the air and backward, away from Jean. His brain felt as if it was exploding.

When he came to, he was lying on the grass outside the main building, with Jean kneeling by his side. She didn't look too good—he could only imagine what *he* looked like. If it was anything like the way he felt, he was in big trouble.

"N-Nate? Nathan? Are you—?"

"I'm not going back," he whispered.

"We have to—" she began to explain. But he cut her off.

"I've had it with the astral plane," he said.

"We can't quit now—"

"Who said anything about quitting?" he

asked her, springing to nis feet. "I'm talking—getting physical!"

Hrrrum! Hrrum!

"Scott! Logan!" Jean screamed over the noise of the weapons blasting. "Get out of there—Cable is opening fire on the laboratory! Stop it, Nate! You'll hit Scott and Logan!"

But Cable kept on firing. "I don't think so, Jean. I know exactly where they are."

And sure enough, two small figures came running toward them out of the rubble that was the laboratory's front wall.

"But what's that behind them?" Cable gasped as a huge quartet of hands rose up, ready to grab the running pair of X-Men.

"Shoot it, Nate!" Jean shouted.

"Gotta cycle the power cells up to full," Cable told her.

The blast was unbelievable. Wolverine and Cyclops were thrown clear, but the hands disintegrated, along with the merged Larissa/Nkotha body they were attached to.

Moments later, the four mutants were reunited. "Scott!" Jean called out as they ran to each other's arms. "Did you find out—?"

"I know where the X-Men are, Jean," he

said. "They're on Chomolungma!"

Wolverine frowned. "Come again?"

"Mount Everest," Cyclops translated. "In Tibet. Eight miles above sea level. But that info cost us," he added grimly. "Moira must have written a failsafe into the operating program. As soon as I accessed the data, the self-destruct timer became active!"

"That's why the Phalanx was trying to absorb the data instead of accessing it!" Cable said. "They were bypassing the—"

"Look!" Jean interrupted, pointing to the ground, where Larissa/Nkotha's remains were moving, rising, reshaping themselves.

"She's pullin' herself back together!" Wolverine said.

"There's less than three minutes left on the timer," Cyclops told them. "After that, this whole island's going to blow—and us along with it."

"At least we take three of them with us," Cable said grimly.

But Wolverine didn't hear him. He was looking skyward, his acute senses alert. "Hear that?" he asked. "Pratt and Whitney engines...it's Harry!"

They could all hear the old plane now, and moments later, it came into view. "That's your ride!" Cable told them. "Go to the headland!"

"We're not leaving you, Cable," Cyclops said to the man who was his son.

"No one is getting away unless someone holds the fort here!" Cable shouted, his left eye glowing orange. "The X-Men need you! I'll slow the Phalanx down and get away on my own! Now go!"

"He's right, Jean," Cyclops said, swallowing hard. "It's the only way!"

"Nate!" Jean called back to him as Scott pulled her away. "W-we'll wait as long as we can!"

"Such a brave act—but so futile!" Larissa/Nkotha reared up above Cable, towering over him, all four hands raised high, ready to strike.

"It isn't over yet," Cable said.

"It is. You knew that when you elected to stay. The others can't be saved, you know. It is only a matter of time before we encompass this entire planet!"

"Not you guys. You're dead meat!"

"We were including you in the collective

pronoun. You are a transmode infectee, after all—already halfway to being one of us! Don't resist the absorption, Cable...it is only delaying the inevitable!"

"*Noooooo!*" Cable screamed, as he felt the psionic wave wash over him. "*Nooooo!*"

"This ain't gonna work, Jean," Wolverine said, watching as the old plane circled low in the sky. It turned to approach them as they stood on the grassy hilltop, near the cliff's edge. "There's no place for him to land!"

"He doesn't have to," Jean explained. "I'm 'telling' him to come in low with the throttle wide open!"

"You're not thinkin' you can—"

"Not think, Logan," Jean interrupted him, her teeth gritted with the incredible mental effort of bringing an entire airplane to a complete stop—in midair! "I...know...I...can!"

"Well!" Wolverine said admiringly as the plane stood motionless in the air before them. "Ain't you just the li'l redhead who could!"

The rear door of the plane opened, and Harry, the pilot, motioned for them to hop on. "That's some trick, lady!" he shouted over the roar of the engines. "Better get on board before this ol' Dakota shakes itself apart!"

But Jean didn't move. Instead, her eyes widened as she picked up a telepathic danger signal. "Wait!" she cried. "It's Nate! The Phalanx is absorbing him!"

"I'll go," Cyclops said to Wolverine.

"You and Jean get on that plane," Wolverine replied, already on the move. "The X-Men are countin' on ya!" And before Cyclops could stop him, Wolverine was gone.

"Go with the flow, Cable! There is much joy in being a part of a greater purpose—it is the true meaning of being whole!"

Cable was down on all fours, breathing heavily, his resistance to the assault of Larissa/Nkotha almost broken.

"I'll give ya a 'hole'!" Wolverine yelled, bursting upon the scene. He slashed the Phalanx unit into pieces with his razor-sharp claws!

"Ya know," he said, as he helped Cable get to his feet, "the big guy might be a royal pain—but he's *our* royal pain! Come on, bub— let's bug out."

"You c-can't stop us! Phalanx can't be stopped!" Larissa/Nkotha screamed in fury as it began to reconstitute itself.

Awoooo-ga! Awoooo-ga!

The siren's blare was deafening. "Rats," Wolverine said as he trudged away with an arm around Cable's waist. "Sounds like our clock just ran out."

And then Muir Island exploded.

"Is everything okay back there?" the pilot called back to his passengers as the explosion hit, rocking the plane. "I don't know how I let you talk me into swinging back around and buzzing that island again. I don't get it! The pressure wave from that explosion should have ripped our airframe to shreds—"

"You did good, Harry," Cyclops told him. "Jean wrapped your plane in a force field—just as she enveloped Nathan and Logan in a psionic cocoon and reeled them in like fish in a trawl net!"

"You got 'em both?" Harry asked, astonished.

"Safe and sound," Jean replied. "And coming aboard even as we speak."

The pilot shook his head in amazement. "Guess I don't have to sing Logan's spirit song for him—this time," he said.

And then, they were aboard, and Cable lay down to recover.

"Nathan, we were worried," Jean told him. "But your techno-organic form has stabilized. It must have been incredibly painful."

"Haven't had much worse," he said weakly.

"Ahem—I'm okay, too," Wolverine spoke up, reminding them of his presence.

"That's great, Logan," Cyclops said absently, totally focused on his son. "You're not bleeding, are you, Cable?"

"Guess I'll mosey up front and see to Harry," Wolverine muttered.

"Look," Cable said, sitting up and looking at them both. "I appreciate the concern. But what the Phalanx did brought back a lot of old memories. If you don't mind, I'd like to be alone for a while."

They did as he asked, joining Wolverine and Harry in the cockpit.

"Set us on a course for Tibet, Harry," Wolverine instructed. "We'll drop you off at the first fuel-stop, and I'll fix it with Xavier to make good on the plane. Gotta save the world, ya know."

"Good luck," Harry said. "From the looks of those things on Muir, you're gonna need it."

And then it became quiet in the cockpit, as everyone looked expectantly to the sky ahead.

⊗ ⊗ ⊗ **13** ⊗ ⊗ ⊗

"Who died and made you two pilots?" Cable griped as the plane rocked and bucked high above the Himalayas. "Are you both trying to get us all killed before we even get to the Phalanx citadel?"

"Lay off 'em, bub," Wolverine ordered gruffly. "They're doin' all right without yer backseat drivin'."

"Butt out, Logan!"

"No, *you* butt out! I've about had it with you, Cable—!"

"The both of you had better lighten up, or I'm going to have to put psionic muzzles on you!" Jean called back from the cockpit.

"Cut us some slack, fellas," Cyclops added. "We've been piloting this antique with the radar and instruments shut down ever since we entered Tibetan airspace!"

"You think that's good enough to escape Phalanx sensors?" Cable asked dubiously.

"They're not expecting anything as low-tech as this fifty-year-old DC-3," Jean pointed out.

"There it is!" Cyclops shouted as he spotted the huge techno-organic web atop the highest mountain in the world.

"Ugly, ain't it?" Wolverine commented. "And big, too—but not so big that we can't crack it!"

"Are you all ready for this?" Cyclops asked. "Remember what's at stake here. We're the last hope. If this desperate measure doesn't suc-ceed—"

"Let's just get on with it!" Wolverine said.

In a hidden room, deep within the citadel, Lang was busy with Psylocke. It seemed as if he was indoctrinating her, trying to break down her will to resist assimilation. But in reality, he had another message altogether to give her—a very secret message.

Do not fight it...let it take over...<*I must communicate with you on a shielded psi-wavelength*>...*The absorption is just a prelude to a boundless ecstasy!*<*You must give no outward indication of this conversation. The others must not suspect! Phalanx has mutated beyond my expectations. I thought they were going to save humanity*—>

<*Not destroy it?*> Psylocke finished for him, speaking on his protected psionic wavelength. <*Why do you say "they"? Are you not one of them?*>

<*I am the interface unit—the one who must remain human to secure our foothold in the human perception of reality!*>

<*Then you still have it, Lang?*>

<*What?*>

<*Your soul!*>

It was at that moment that Hodge interrupted their conversation. "Lang! We have a security anomaly—an unidentified aircraft has penetrated our sensor screen!"

"What? Impossible! You know we are able to detect the most sophisticated electronic

arrays and all manner of passive cloaking devices—"

"It is emitting no radar or infrared or even microwaves—as if it were some sort of primitive, pre-nuclear device—it's going to hit us! *Reformat!* Spread the citadel away from the point of impact!"

The sudden intrusion of twenty-six thousand pounds of steel and aluminum traveling at three hundred miles per hour would be traumatic by itself—but the fuel tanks had been opened by psionic means to spill high-octane aviation fuel across the wing surfaces and fuselage. The result was explosive, to say the least.

When the reverberations of the huge blast had faded, Hodge looked around the smoke-filled web. "Lang! Where are you?"

"I am safe, Hodge."

"The mutants must be desperate if they are resorting to suicide attacks! I must see to the reorganization of the collective for damage control, Lang. Did the explosion terminate the subject designated: Psylocke?"

"No. She survived, and still functions as a carbonite entity."

"Not for long. It's too bad we can't assimi-late these filthy mutants as easily as we co-opt the pathetic humans!"

The being who was once Dr. Steven Lang pretended to agree, but his hidden inner con-sciousness was enraged.

He could see now where the Phalanx was headed. It was now trying to create an Earth empty of all life forms except its own.

Lang had to stop them.

He had hidden all he knew from Hodge, including the fact that the mutants who were in the plane were still alive!

A thousand feet below the citadel, on the north face of the mountain, the four mutants were now scaling a towering vertical cliff.

"You must have spent your whole honey-moon practicing, Jean," Cable said as he helped her onto a ledge, "to spot a two-foot-wide ledge from a speeding plane half a mile away—and put us this close to it!"

"I was aiming for one a lot closer to the citadel, Nathan," she replied.

"You did fine, Jean," Cyclops said. "We're outside the range of their localized psi-scans."

"In other words," Cable said, "we're sneak-ing up on their blind side."

"Got a lot o' experience with that, huh?" Wolverine growled.

"We could settle our differences right now, Logan," Cable threatened.

"You know you won't do it, bub," Wolverine replied. "This mission is too impor-tant. The team comes first."

"It always has, Logan," Cable said.

"So what now, Cable?" Wolverine asked. "You're the mission leader on this fiasco—why don't ya just bodyslide up into the Phalanx nest and drop a rope down for the rest of us? An' while we climb up, you can run amok with that gun o' yours..."

"That's too dangerous," Jean interrupted. "Nathan's techno-organics make him too vul-nerable to absorption by himself! If they assimilate him, they'll know everything we know."

"Furthermore," Cyclops added, "if Cable or Jean or any of us were to use our mutant pow-ers, Phalanx would detect us immediately!"

"No way around it, then," Cable said, gath-ering the rope. "It's fingers and toes, handhold by handhold, crevice to crevice—straight up, one thousand feet!"

"Piece o' cake, bub!" Wolverine said with a wry grin.

"Right," Cable said. And they began to climb.

Inside, Hodge and Lang stood in the chamber where the imprisoned X-Men lay, each of them surrounded by techno-organic cocoons.

"I cannot understand it, Lang. If we cannot absorb these mutants, we should terminate them! They may yet find a way to escape from the magnetic fields that imprison them."

"We need living specimens if we are to solve the problem, Hodge."

Deep in the hidden part of Lang's mind, ideas were being formed—and rejected. Each plan meant freeing the X-Men—the very group of mutants he had once set out to destroy!

Hodge was standing over the cocoon that held Bishop. "At the very least, we should nullify this one! He is an energy drainer! Think of the havoc he would wreak if—"

"Go see to external security, Hodge. This is

my area of expertise."

"I don't believe that the X-Men would crash into the citadel on purpose, thinking they could destroy it that way! I will run a scan down the mountain."

"Don't bother with the north face, Hodge. It is unclimbable."

They were coming. Lang knew it. But were they strong enough to overcome Hodge and the collective Phalanx units? Would he be able to help them? No—putting up blocks and walls to hide his thoughts took too much energy, and—

Wait. Walls! That was the key! Now he knew what he had to do. With Hodge still watching, Lang turned to Psylocke.

"You are going to submerge your consciousness and allow an override system to assume command." *<This procedure will be impossible without your complete cooperation, Psylocke—you'll have to trust me—you'll have no protection of your own! >*

"The override system will be pre-programmed with an attack agenda."*<You will be totally vulnerable to complete absorption, but it is the only way to place you where you can help the other X–Men! >*

"Your main target will be Cable, and your

mission will be his complete assimilation into the Phalanx." *<But I am creating a wall within the override that will be triggered by your attack on Cable. This will free you to help the X-Men. Do you trust me enough to submit? Will you do it?>*

"There's no way I will submit to that!" Psylocke answered for Hodge's benefit. But on the private wavelength, she added, *<I don't trust you. But I have no choice. Go ahead.>*

He gave her a long look. *<Your first order of business will be to betray Hodge.>*

"This would be impossible for a normal human," Cable said as they climbed the sheer face of the cliff, "and nearly impossible for a mutant in top shape. I know you haven't been up to snuff lately, Logan—so if you need a hand, just let me know!"

"My adamantium skeleton may be gone," Wolverine grunted as he climbed, "my healin' factor may be a little faded, and my body may be feelin' its age—but there sure ain't nothin' wrong with my will! Keep climbin', bub. I'll keep up."

Jean, Cyclops said silently, sending her his thoughts, *I look at Cable, and all I see is the child we spent ten years raising in the future! I'm afraid for him, Jean!*

No parent should ever have to go into battle with their own child by their side, she agreed. *It's hard enough to do your own job in the heat of a fight..*

Suddenly, they could climb no higher—an overhanging ledge completely blocked their path!

"Looks like this is the end of the line!" Cable shouted down to them. "This overhang stretches all the way across this face! It'd be tough enough if we had hooks and ice-hammers, but with bare hands—not easy!"

"Get outta the way an' let me take a whack at it," Wolverine demanded.

"Think you're Spider-Man, Logan?" Cable asked. "Guts and bullheadedness can't overcome gravity! But if Jean were to use her psi-power to push me out and up, I could grab the edge of the overhang—"

"Phalanx would be on us in no time!" Wolverine finished for him.

"Not necessarily," Cyclops interjected.

"You got an idea, Scott?" Cable asked.

"What if Jean limited herself to a short

concentrated burst? It would have to be accurate, and there's no second chance—if Cable misses and falls, we'll have to let him go or endanger the mission and thereby doom the rest of the world! But a short burst might go by Phalanx undetected."

"Scott!" Jean gasped. "What are you asking me to do?"

He looked back at her grimly. "We don't have any choice," he said.

"What's your problem?" Cable asked her. "After all, it's not as if you were the one who used to toss me up in the air when I was a toddler!" He looked at her meaningfully—as if he were looking right through her.

"No, that was somebody else, wasn't it?" Jean answered, panicked. "Redd? She used to toss you up."

The memories flooded back over both of them. But they were remembrances of things yet to come—glimpses of a future still unborn.

"Jean," Cable broke off the moment. "We're losing time."

"You can do it," Cyclops told her. "I'm right here with you."

"I'm ready when you are," Cable said.

Jean took a deep breath. "Stretch for it!" she cried. *"Now!"*

"Lang! Did you feel that? There are mutants on the mountain! The plane was but a diversion!"

"Where are these mutant intruders, Hodge? Can you locate them?"

"They're on the north face!"

"Impossible."

"I tell you, Lang, there are mutants scaling the north face! I felt a burst of energy—"

"That is an illogical assertion, Hodge. The north face is impossible—"

"Impossible to normal humans! These are mutants, and they are either masking their powers or they are deliberately not using them!"

"Hodge, you have stated yourself that the mutants can't use their mutant powers, or we will sense them—that reduces them to normal human level, and normal humans can't climb the north face! If you insist on seeing with your own eyes—"

"No. Your reasoning is sound, Lang. I will conduct a physical scan of our perimeter.

Perhaps my readings have been tampered with by mutant interference. Perhaps they are coming some other way..."

"Uhh..." Cable grunted, his grip slipping. "Didn't realize the upper surface sloped! Angle's too steep!"

"Nathan!" Jean screamed, about to use her powers to help him.

"No!" Cable shouted down to her. "Don't do it! Not yet!" His fingers dug into the soil, and at least for the moment, stopped his slide.

"Hang on tight, Twinkle-face!" Wolverine yelled, leaping and grabbing Cable's legs. "Here comes the Canucklehead! Hope ya got those fingers dug in real good!"

"They'll hold!" Cable shouted as Wolverine climbed over him toward the top of the ledge.

"I'll reach over the top and secure a rope!" Wolverine told him. Quickly, he managed it, and helped Jean and Cyclops scramble up after him. Then he reached down to pull Cable up. "Gimme yer hand, big guy."

Cable grabbed it. "Hope you had your Wheaties this mornin', Logan."

"Listen up, Cable," he said, in a low voice

that only Cable could hear. "I never saw Jean look as scared as she did when she thought you was takin' the long drop. You hear what I'm sayin'? That lady back there is real special to me. And it sure looks like you're real special to her. So as far as I'm concerned, the slate is clean between us. But if you ever break her heart, I'm gonna deal with you myself."

With that, he hauled Cable up. The two glared at each other silently for a long moment. And then, they turned around to find that they were on top of the mountain— at the walls of the Phalanx citadel.

The Phalanx units were startled to see Psylocke walking freely among them.

"What is the absorption designate doing walking about free? Brick, Dymphna, restrain her and—"

"There is no need. You can verify with a scan—"

Hodge walked over to examine her. "You have submitted to an override program! You are no longer consciously resisting the absorption process?"

"As you can see," she replied, "I am now a

totally submissive pre-programmed tool of the collective consciousness. As such, I must regretfully report that Lang has partitioned his own consciousness and is blocking certain unknown thoughts from the general pool!"

Hodge gaped at her in disbelief. "Impossible! That would be a deviation in logic—he would not risk betraying himself by reformatting this absorption designate."

Hodge turned away from her, and back to the task at hand—the wreckage of the airplane.

"Why reconstruct the aircraft, Hodge?"

"There is always a chance that we overlooked a clue...Aha! The remains of a techno-organic tendril! This aircraft must have been on Muir Island! It contains memory! Or at least fragments of memory. Now, we can find out!"

Nearby, in the heart of the citadel, Lang watched the imprisoned X-Men with intense interest. They were closing in on the endgame. Now was the time for precise and deliberate moves.

Ah...the one called Bishop was straining at

his prison. Did he know? It would be so easy if Lang could simply free them all! But the cocoons they were in were held together by all the Phalanx as a unit—just as they all held the entire citadel together.

If anything were to disturb the field, all the Phalanx entities would know immediately. No. There had to be another way—but how could he even let the attacking X-Men know that he was willing to aid them?

"I got us up here, Cyclops," Cable said. "I hope your plan for this attack works!"

"It should, Nathan. Let's go over it once more. I blast a hole through the bottom of the citadel, and Jean tele-flings Nathan and me up through the breach. We go in blasting. Jean follows up with a concentrated psi-attack. But it is up to Cable and me to lead this charge. You know what to do, Logan?"

"Let's get on with it," Wolverine said.

"Here goes!" With that, Cyclops leveled an optic blast at the citadel wall. A huge hole opened in it, and he and Cable ran in.

"Be careful, both of you!" Jean called after them.

"We ain't winnin' this shootin' match by tiptoein' through the tulips, darlin'," Wolverine reminded her as they followed the others inside.

There, Cable and Cyclops blasted away at the defenders. The Phalanx units quickly surrounded them and pressed forward, only to be thrown back by the sudden force of the mutant assault.

"They're coming out of the walls!" Cyclops shouted as more and more Phalanx units advanced on them.

"They *are* the walls!" Cable retorted.

"Mutants! Genetic anomalies are within the citadel!"

"We gotta move out!" Cable yelled as the Phalanx units pressed forward. "You take the point, Cyclops!"

"This way!" Cyclops shouted, beckoning. "Jean! Back us up!"

"Disengage! Regroup! Hodge! Where are you?"

Hodge's eyes glowed with red-hot fury. "The mutant filth have invaded the citadel. The citadel has been entered on the lowest level along the north face—and Lang was insistent that we ignore the north face! I will absorb Lang myself!" he told the others. "I will destroy his consciousness!"

"And I hope you choke," Wolverine muttered under his breath as he watched Hodge stalk away. The path was momentarily clear. Now was his chance. "Here goes nothin'!"

⊗ ⊗ ⊗ **14** ⊗ ⊗ ⊗

In an interior chamber, Wolverine's companions found themselves surrounded.

"Close off all exits from the main atrium! We have the mutants trapped! Surround them and eliminate them! The Phalanx cannot be stopped! We are the answer!"

Hodge, too, had been sidetracked in his search for Lang, and was battling it out with the three mutants. "Be wary—these mutants are dangerous! Do not underestimate their prowess!"

"Jean! Scott!" Cable shouted, as his companions were battered by body blows.

"Relinquish yourself, Cable!" Hodge said. "You are halfway to being ours anyway! Merge with the new order and be absorbed into virtual immortality!"

"So who wants to live forever?" Cable asked, smashing Hodge with a swipe of his metallic arm.

"Eeeeeeeeeeee! Deconstruct him!"

"Can't take a joke, huh?" Cable asked, leveling his blaster.

In the heart of the citadel, Wolverine found the X-Men, unguarded. The Phalanx units had all gone down to the lower level of the north face to fight the invasion of their citadel.

"What is this stuff?" he asked himself as he chopped away at the cocoon that held Bishop. "It's tougher than rhino hide! Maybe if I just keep chippin' away at the same spot, it'll wear away enough for me to rip through it!"

He leveled another swipe, and felt it give. "That did somethin' to it, but not too all-fired much!"

"You've done it, Logan," Bishop said from

within the cocoon. "You have freed us!"

"Ain't no more than a pinhole, Bishop!"

"It will be enough!"

"Hodge! Do you feel that?"

"Yessss! The containment fields in the womb! The X-Men are escaping! Brick and Dymphna, see to the mutant prisoners in their stasis fields. Terminate their life functions if necessary!"

It was only moments before Wolverine found himself surrounded. "Now we got 'em oozin' outta the walls!" he exclaimed.

"Remember the plan, Logan!" Bishop urged.

"Don't bug me, Bishop! I'll keep up my end o' the deal! C'mon, ya ugly yahoos!"

"Logan—deflect them to me!"

"How's this?" Wolverine asked, throwing a Phalanx unit Bishop's way.

"Perfect! All I need is one point of contact to absorb all their energy!"

With a loud *pop,* the cocoon and the Phalanx unit both exploded. Bishop emerged, scowling and ready for battle. "Help me,

Logan," he said. "We must free the others!"

"What's holding up that little hairball?" Cable wondered. "We are down to the wire here—"

"Lighten up, Cable!" Wolverine shouted as he entered the chamber at the head of their freed companions. "The X-Men are here, and we're ready for action!"

"A l'attacque!" Gambit roared in his New Orleans French accent.

"I wouldn't put it so crudely, Gambit," Beast said with a grin. "Let's pummel these louts!"

"Yeah, what you guys said," Wolverine agreed. "Come on!"

Hodge watched in disbelief and fury as he suddenly found his minions outnumbered by mutants. "Psylocke—can you hear me?"

"Yes, Hodge."

"Attack the X-Men!"

"All the X-Men?"

"Concentrate on Cable first, then—"

Suddenly, Psylocke shuddered. "That's the trigger!" she cried, striking out with her psychic knife and felling two Phalanx units. "The override system has been dumped! I am free to help the X-Men! Jean and Cable, channel your psi-energies through me!"

"I'm giving it all I've got!" Cable shouted.

"I see what you're doing, Psylocke!" Jean called to her. "You're funneling our combined psi-powers, concentrating them all on a focal point—to destroy the Phalanx psi-net! Without their psionic communication link, they are unconnected entities—unable to function!"

And then it was done. Hodge, cut loose from the collective consciousness, seethed with rage. For a flashing moment, during Psylocke's psi-blast, her memories were open, and he had seen—"It was Lang! He set this all up! He has betrayed the Phalanx!"

"Lang can't really be on our side!" Jean gasped.

"I doubt it," said Psylocke, as they continued to do battle with the isolated Phalanx units. "There were blocks within blocks, and who knows? Perhaps I am even now being used to further Lang's aims—whatever they are!"

"It's all over!" Cable said. "Look at your skin, Hodge. The techno-web is starting to dissolve. Bishop is absorbing the remaining Phalanx energy. And when he lets go, it'll be real explosive!"

"Phalanx is not beaten yet! We have reserves that are as of yet untapped! I can access the Phalanx global net and drain the power from our nests in Paris...London... Tokyo...and the rest of the Earth! The massive power drain will destroy the nests and all the Phalanx entities within them. But what do they matter if the citadel and our collective consciousness are no more?"

And as the X-Men looked on in horror, Hodge began to grow—and grow—and grow!

From a short distance away, outside the citadel, Lang watched as the battle raged. He had seen the truth in time. Now he could destroy the Phalanx and survive to start all over again. Next time, he would destroy all mutantkind and save humanity from their polluting curse.

Hodge had done what he expected. He had drawn the power from the nests, and eradicated every Phalanx outpost on the planet! But it was too late—because now, he, Lang, could rid the Earth of the remainder of the Phalanx.

Hodge had probably already forgotten that Lang had taken over the entire task of psionically holding together the citadel! It would now be a simple matter to let go—and to allow it to plummet from the highest peak in creation!

"The citadel is collapsing!" Storm cried. "Jean, envelop all the non-flying X-Men in a psionic field. I will call up a mighty gale to hold them against the rock face of the mountain!"

"It's working, Storm!" Jean called back to her as they put their plan into action. All around them, the citadel was slipping away, carrying the remaining Phalanx units with it!

"Lang!" Hodge shrieked as he fell. "I shall not perish alone!"

Extending a long tentacle, he grabbed Lang, pulling him down along with the entire Phalanx citadel. "No!" Lang screamed. "Hodge—you don't know what you're doing! *Aaiiieeeeee!*"

The X-Men looked on in wonder as the Phalanx citadel disappeared down the mountainside, falling into oblivion.

"Looks like the whole Phalanx is taking the long ride down the steep side of Everest!" Wolverine said with satisfaction.

"How many living, thinking entities were in there, Jean?" Storm asked. "Are they still a psionic presence?"

"Oh, Storm," Jean replied with a sad sigh. "They are like lights, blinking out one by one..."

"Don't feel too sorry for them," Cable said. "Remember what they were trying to do!"

Jean shook off the feeling, and then contacted Professor X telepathically, to let him know what had happened.

"That's wonderful news, Jean," Xavier told her. "And Banshee, Emma Frost, and Jubilee succeeded in rescuing the next generation of young mutants, as well. But something most peculiar has happened—the other X-teams had pinpointed and targeted the other Phalanx centers worldwide. Now, it appears the centers have suddenly disintegrated!"

Jean smiled. "I think I know why, Professor. But it's a long, long story. Let's talk about it back at the X-Mansion—soon!"

"Amen to that, darlin'!" Wolverine said. He threw an arm around Jean's shoulder, and another around Cable's. "Let's go home, everybody. I don't know about you, but I'm kinda tired. I think it's time for a little vacation! Anyone wanna join me?"

All the X–Men let out a cheer. A vacation was one thing they could all agree on—and did they ever deserve it!

He's turbo-charged and ready for action...

"He's waking up, Doc. More tranquilizers?"

"Not necessary. I'm tying off the last suture now."

"Huh? What the—?" Creed awoke to a blinding pain. His eyelids were held open with clamps and his whole body was spread out on an X-shaped operating table. Metal cuffs held down his wrists and his ankles, so that even if he could move—if the pain didn't feel as if it was ripping his whole body apart—it would be impossible for him to hurt anyone or anything. A man in glasses and a surgical mask leaned over him.

"Don't strain, Sabretooth," came a voice from the other side of the room. "You'll pop your stitches. Doctor Mabuse has been working around the clock for the last week, giving you a full system upgrade. You can now consider yourself to be Turbo-Sabretooth."

"You made me stronger?" Sabretooth grunted.

It wasn't a lot of fun getting stitched up without anesthesia. He raised his head high enough to get a glimpse of what the doctor was doing. From the looks of it, his body was one big road-map of incisions. Nice job.

"That was pretty stupid," Sabretooth growled. "You know what I'm gonna do when I—"

"We also installed a control device next to your aorta," the voice went on. "I'll come to that in a minute."

"Who are ya?" Creed demanded. "Show your face so I can get a good look at it before I smash it into a million pieces."

A robotic figure approached the operating table. From what Creed could tell, the figure was actually a man inside a huge green suit of armor. He wore a helmet that prevented Creed from seeing his face.

"I am Tribune," the man said. "And I have had all of this done to you so you will be able to carry out a very special assassination."

"Calling me on the phone wasn't enough, huh?" said Creed through gritted teeth. "I guess ya wanted to give me the job in person. That was a nice thought, but I coulda told you on the phone: I don't work for guys in big green robot suits. It ain't my style."

Tribune ignored him. "The control device I mentioned earlier is to ensure that you carry out this little mission. I don't expect you to take my word as to the effectiveness of this device. Bring in the ninja."

Creed raised his head from the operating table, grimacing from the effort. He looked up long enough to see one of his old red-robed pals from outside his mansion, a Clan Yashida guy. Was it just last night that he'd been ambushed by ninjas? How long had he been living this prison hospital nightmare?

"My employees found this skulker lurking in your rosebushes," Tribune said, confirming Creed's suspicions. "I had a control device implanted in his chest as well. For purposes of demonstration," he added coldly.

Tribune raised his hand to show Creed the remote he was holding. He pressed his thumb on the remote's red button. There was a *bleep*. And then the ninja blew apart—into a thousand tiny pieces.

Fast forward—2,000 years!

"All right," Jean said, glancing around her. She tried to remain calm as she clung to the end of a jagged-edged structure. "I'm totally confused. One minute we're lounging on the shores of St. Bart's, having the ultimate honeymoon. The next minute, I'm alone in the middle of nowhere!"

Then she saw him, across a wide chasm, hanging precariously from a giant platform. Could it be...

"Scott!" Jean gasped, still straining to hold on. She realized he couldn't hear her. So she tried to contact him telepathically. *Scott?*

Where are we? came Scott's reply as he hauled himself up onto the platform. *This techno-organic complex is unfamiliar to me. And what are we doing in these bodies?*

Scott *did* look totally different. He was older and plainer, with wavy light brown hair and more thickset features than his own. Until that moment, it hadn't occurred to Jean that she might look like a whole new person, too.

It seems that, despite everything, we've maintained our psionic bond, she told him.

I suppose it makes sense, he replied silently. *Whoever placed us in these bodies filled them with our essences. You and I were a part of each other long before we got married.*

But there was no time to think about that now, with explosions echoing all around them. And an army rushing about below them.

Their telepathic conversation was suddenly interrupted by one of the soldiers below. "Sir," he cried out urgently. "I'm bio-scanning two survivors!"

Uh-oh, Jean flashed to Scott. *Looks like we've been discovered.*

"Where?" the commander shouted.

"There!" the soldier said, pointing straight up at Scott and Jean. "In the rafters!"

The commander looked up and saw them.

"Ah, yes," he said, his eyes narrowing. "Right you are, soldier. They are survivors—but not for long!"